EVERYBODY

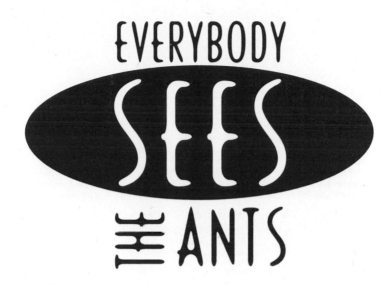

SEES

THE ANTS

WITHDRAWN

a novel by

A.S. King

LITTLE, BROWN AND COMPANY
New York   Boston

Little, Brown and Company

Hachette Book Group
237 Park Avenue, New York, NY 10017
Visit our website at www.lb-teens.com

Little, Brown and Company is a division of Hachette Book Group, Inc.
The Little, Brown name and logo are trademarks of Hachette Book Group, Inc.

The publisher is not responsible for websites (or their content) that are not owned by the publisher.

First Edition: October 2011

The characters and events portrayed in this book are fictitious. Any similarity to real persons,
living or dead, is coincidental and not intended by the author.

Library of Congress Cataloging-in-Publication Data

King, A. S. (Amy Sarig), 1970–
    Everybody sees the ants / by A.S. King. — 1st ed.
        p. cm.
    Summary: Overburdened by his parents' bickering and a bully's attacks, fifteen-year-old
Lucky Linderman begins dreaming of being with his grandfather, who went missing during the Vietnam War, but during a visit to Arizona, his aunt and uncle and their beautiful
neighbor, Ginny, help him find a new perspective.
    ISBN 978-0-316-12928-2
    [1. Self-confidence—Fiction.   2. Family problems—Fiction.   3. Bullies—Fiction.
4. Dreams—Fiction.   5. Grandfathers—Fiction.   6. Missing persons—Fiction.   7. Vietnam
War, 1961–1975—Fiction.   8. Arizona—Fiction.]   I. Title.
    PZ7.K5693Eve 2012
    [Fic]—dc22   2010049434

10 9 8 7 6 5 4 3 2 1

RRD-C

Printed in the United States of America

Book design by Saho Fujii

For everybody
who sees the ants.

PART ONE

Who can stop the tears?
—*Robert Nesta Marley*

OPERATION DON'T SMILE
EVER — FRESHMAN YEAR

All I did was ask a stupid question.

Six months ago I was assigned the standard second-semester freshman social studies project at Freddy High: Create a survey, evaluate data, graph data, express conclusion in a two-hundred-word paper. This was an easy A. I thought up my question and printed out 120 copies.

The question was: *If you were going to commit suicide, what method would you choose?*

This was a common conversation topic between Nader (shotgun in the mouth), Danny (jump in front of a speeding truck) and me (inhaling car fumes), and we'd been joking about it for months during seventh-period study hall. I never saw anything bad in it. That kind of stuff made Nader laugh.

And Nader laughing at my jokes meant maybe I could get through high school with less shrapnel.

When I told the principal that day that it was a joke between Danny, Nader and me, he rolled his eyes and told me that Danny and Nader were not having "social problems" at Freddy High.

"But *you*, Mr. Linderman, *are.*"

Apparently, Evelyn Schwartz went blabbing to the guidance counselor about my questionnaire. She said it was "morbid" and "creepy." (Evelyn Schwartz has a T-shirt that says HE DIED FOR ME with a picture of a dead guy nailed to a cross on it. Oh, the irony.) I really don't think it's that morbid of a thing to ask. I'm pretty sure everybody has thought about it at one time or another. My whole plan was to make a few cool pie charts or bar graphs, you know — to show off my Microsoft Excel skills with labels such as SLIT WRISTS, OVERDOSE and FIREARMS. Anyway, just because a person talks about suicide does not make it a "cry for help." Even if the kid's a little bit short or unpopular compared to his so-called friends.

Three hours after my meeting with the principal, I was sitting in the guidance office. Six days later, I was in the conference room with my parents, surrounded by the school district's "experts" who watched my every move and scribbled notes about my behavior. In the end they recommended family therapy, suggested medications and further professional testing for disorders like depression, ADHD and Asperger's syndrome. Professional testing! For asking a dumb question about how you'd off yourself if you were going to off yourself.

It's as if they'd never known one single teenager in their whole lives.

My parents were worse. They just sat there acting as if the "experts" knew me better than they did. The more I watched Mom jiggle her leg and Dad check his watch, the more I realized maybe that was true. Maybe complete strangers *did* know me better than they did.

And seriously — if one more person explained to me how "precious" my life was, I was going to puke. This was Evelyn's word, straight from her mega-hard-core church group: *Precious*. Precious life.

I said, "Why didn't anyone think my life was precious when I told them Nader McMillan was pushing me around? That was...what? Second grade? Fifth grade? Seventh grade? Every freaking year of my life?" I didn't mention the day before in the locker room, but I was thinking about it.

"There's no need to get hostile, Lucky," one of them said. "We're just trying to make sure you're okay."

"Do I look okay to you?"

"There's no need for sarcasm either," Jerk-off #2 said. "Sometimes it's hard to grasp just how precious life *is* at your age."

I laughed. I didn't know what else to do.

Jerk-off #1 asked me, "Do you think this is funny? Joking about killing yourself?"

And I said yes. Of course, none of us knew then that the suicide questionnaires were going to come back completed. And when they did, I wouldn't be telling any of these people, that's for sure. I mean, there they were, asking me if *I* was okay when they're letting people like Nader run around and calling him *normal*. Just because he *seems* okay and because he can pin a guy's shoulders to the mat in under a minute doesn't mean he's not cornering kids in the locker room and doing things to them you don't want to think about. Because he did. I saw him do it and I saw him laughing.

They asked me to wait in the guidance lobby, and I sat in the tweed chair closest to the door, where I could hear them talking to my leg-jiggling, watch-checking parents. Apparently, smiling and joking was an additional sign that I needed "real help."

And so I initiated Operation Don't Smile Ever. It's been a very successful operation. We have perplexed many an enemy.

THE FIRST THING YOU NEED
TO KNOW—THE SQUID

My mother is addicted to swimming. I don't mean this in a cute, doing-handstands-in-the-shallow-end sort of way. I mean she's *addicted*—more than two hundred laps a day, no matter what. So I'm spending this summer vacation, like pretty much every summer vacation I can remember, at the Frederickstown Community Swimming Pool. Operation Don't Smile Ever is still in full effect. I haven't smiled in six months.

Mom told me once she thinks she's a reincarnated squid. Maybe she thinks being a squid means she won't be swallowed by the hole in our family. Maybe being submerged in 250,000 gallons of water all the time makes the hole more comfortable. I heard her yelling at Dad again last night.

"You call this trying?"

"See? Nothing's ever good enough," Dad said.

"I dare you to come home and actually see us every damn day in one damn week."

"I can do that."

"Starting when?"

After a brief silence he said, "You know, maybe if you weren't such a nag, I'd want to be around more often."

The door slammed soon after that, and I was happy he'd left. I don't like hearing him call her a nag when anyone can see she does what he tells her to do all the time. *Don't talk to him about that Nader kid, Lori. It'll just make him embarrassed. And whatever you do, don't call the principal. That'll get him beat up worse.*

The Freddy pool isn't so bad — at least when Nader McMillan isn't around. Even when he *is* around, working his one or two lifeguarding shifts a week, he's usually too distracted by his hot lifeguard girlfriend to pay attention to me. So, for the most part, it's a quiet, friendly neighborhood pool experience.

Mom and I leave home at ten, eat a packed lunch in the shade at one and get back home at six, where there is a 92 percent chance we will eat without Dad and an 8 percent chance he'll take a break from working at the fancy-schmancy restaurant and come home to eat with us and say things like, "Do you think that berry compote works with the chicken?" Mom says she's glad Dad's a chef, because it makes him happy. She only says this to make me feel better about never seeing him. She makes herself feel better by swimming laps.

While Mom worships her pool god, I shoot hoops or play box hockey. I read a book in the shade or play cards with Lara Jones. I eat. The snack bar's mozzarella sticks are really good as long as Danny Hoffman isn't working, because Danny is an idiot and he turns the fryer temperature up so the food cooks faster, but the middles of the sticks are still frozen.

Danny can be cool outside of the snack bar, and he sometimes plays a game of H-O-R-S-E or Around the World with me on the basketball court. He still hangs out with Nader McMillan, but only because Nader would kill him if he didn't stay on his good side.

I used to hang out with Nader sometimes, too, because of Danny, even after all the crappy shit Nader did to me, but that was before my famous freshman year social studies suicide-questionnaire screwup, when he decided to make my life a living hell again.

Today I didn't bring a book, and I don't feel like playing basketball or box hockey. Mom is out there by herself, swimming in lane three, occasionally eyeing the menacing clouds that are approaching from the west. I'm left lying here on our beach blanket in the shade, daydreaming. Sometimes I daydream myself to sleep and into my dreams. Sometimes I just close my eyes and pretend I'm a sniper, like my granddad Harry was in Vietnam. I imagine Nader in my sights, crosshairs on his forehead. Every day I kill him.

My mother could swim right through a thunderstorm, but they won't let her.

"Let's go stand under the pavilion until it clears," she says.

I sit down at the picnic table across from Lara Jones, a fellow fifteen-year-old soon-to-be-sophomore from my school who has a mild case of summer acne. A lightning bolt strikes over by the basketball court, and we brace ourselves for the clap. It rattles the tin roof of the pavilion, and Lara shivers.

"Wanna play cards?" she asks me.

"Sure."

"Gin?"

"Yeah. Ten card. No knocks," I say, because I hate all those stupid extra rules.

"I'll still beat you," she says.

"Winning isn't everything," I say.

She grins at me. "Sure it isn't."

The rain comes down hard while Lara and I play gin. She beats me two out of three before the rain stops and I head over to the snack bar.

"What do you want?" Danny asks. So I ask him for a fifteen-cent bag of Swedish Fish.

"Multicolored or red?"

"Red, please."

He mocks me, "*Red, please.* God, Linderman, you're such a mama's boy."

I said hello to him at the mall last week, and he said the same thing: *Stop being such a mama's boy, Linderman.* I liked the old Danny more—the Danny who used to play Transformers with me in our adjoining backyards. The Danny who wasn't trying to prove anything.

He hands me a twist-tied plastic bag of Swedish Fish. "So are you gonna ask her out?"

I feign an expression of repulsion. "Lara Jones?"

"If you aren't, I will."

"Why?" I ask. I know Danny isn't into Lara Jones.

"My brother says ugly girls give out faster."

Fact is, I'd ask Lara out if I knew how to do it. But I don't know how to do it.

Dad is actually home when we get back from the pool. He says to Mom, "See? I'm *here*." After a near-silent dinner (grilled pork loin with raspberries and garlic potatoes), Dad asks me if I want to watch TV with him, and he turns on the Food Channel, which is the only channel he watches.

Tonight's special is about Cajun food, followed by two episodes of *FMC*, which is *The Five-Minute Challenge*. Five chefs have to pick five ingredients (out of ten) and invent a meal in five minutes. The meal must be ready to serve twenty minutes after the clock starts. Dad doesn't let me talk during the show. I'm allowed to talk during commercials, but I don't.

Dad sits in his green corduroy chair and balances the remote on its arm. I'm spread out on the couch with my arms behind my head. My eyelids get heavy, and I can't keep my eyes open past the first *FMC* episode. I have half dreams about gumbo-flavored ice cream and Lara Jones playing gin, until I hear the door close behind Dad, who left for the restaurant the minute he thought I was sleeping.

THE SECOND THING YOU NEED TO KNOW—
NADER McMILLAN

The thunderstorms yesterday did not clear the humidity, as predicted. Petra Simmons, Nader McMillan's girlfriend-for-the-summer, is in the diving-well guard chair, wearing a navy blue sporty bikini. She's the color of peanut butter, holding a red float across her perfect legs. I usually can't look at her without getting an instant boner, but today it's even too humid to get a boner.

I do a cannonball and try to splash her.

When I surface, she says, "Feels great! Do it again!"

I aim my next splash at the guard chair, and when I look, I see Petra is rubbing the droplets of water into her arms and legs. This is probably the hottest thing that's ever happened to me in relation to a girl. So I hop up the steps and onto the board again.

I look out over the Freddy pool. My mother is over in lane three and her stroke looks choppy and annoyed by the increasing amount of people in her way. Two of them are so involved in making out that Mom has to stop mid-stroke and wait until they drift into lane two. The make-out couple is skimpy-bikini-clad Charlotte Dent, a senior next year, and her new, twenty-year-old townie boyfriend, Ronald, who has a mustache and a red-tailed hawk tattooed across his chest, muscular shoulder to muscular shoulder. He works at the battery factory six days a week. Today must be his day off, which means he'll leave for lunch soon and come back with a six-pack of beer and proceed to drink it in the parking lot with Charlotte. Today she's wearing the leopard-skin string bikini, and I have to look away when she gets out of the pool, to avoid thinking too intensely about her nipples.

After two more cannonballs I come up for air, and Nader McMillan is sitting on the edge of the pool, next to the ladder.

He leans down to my water-filled ear. "So you wanna stick your little wiener in my girlfriend, do ya?"

"No."

"Why don't you go back to your mom and stick it in her?"

I look over. She's doing a lap of breaststroke with one eye on me. While my head is turned, Nader pushes the back of my skull playfully, but enough to make my head lurch forward and bounce off the ladder handle. I swim to the other ladder, ten feet away, and climb out of the water and walk over to our blanket.

Two minutes after I spread out on the blanket and open

the paperback I'm reading, the yelling starts. I see Nader and his friends still over by the diving board. Petra's in the chair. Nader is shouting and pointing. There's movement in the water, but I can't see who or what it is, so I get up and start to walk slowly toward the edge of the pool.

"Don't help her!" Nader says.

Petra is standing on the chair's step now, whistle in mouth, pointing at Nader.

"Let her get it herself!" he yells.

Petra toots her whistle at Nader and gives him the *what are you doing?* look with her hands out and her head tilted. He totally blows her off.

She blows her whistle again. Meekly. "Come on. Just stop."

Nader ignores her again and starts laughing at whoever is splashing in the pool. I move close enough to see it's Charlotte — and she's missing her leopard-skin bikini top.

"Come out," Nader taunts. "You little slut."

I squint at the twelve-foot-deep diving well and see a vague shadow at the bottom.

"If one of you doesn't get it, I will," Petra says, now motioning for another guard to help out. I look around for hawk-tattooed Ronald. His car isn't in the parking lot.

"Lighten up, Pet. We're just having some fun. She's a slut, right? She probably *wants* us to see her boobs," Nader says.

That's the last thing I hear before I swim across the pool toward the diving well. Petra isn't helping because Nader is her boyfriend. None of the other guards are helping because they're all afraid of him, like everyone else in this town. Charlotte is hanging on to the concrete gutter of the pool with one hand while the other is clamped across her chest.

"Hey!" Nader shouts, right before I dive to the bottom.

It's dark this deep, and something about it makes me feel calm. Something about the pressure on my eardrums and that feeling in the back of my throat. Something about the brilliant cerulean blue of the water down here makes me feel welcome. It's like I'm more comfortable twelve feet deep than I am on land, especially after the last stupid, horrible six months of my life.

I come up with the bikini top and swim over to Charlotte. She slips it over her head and dives under the ropes to the shallower lanes, where I help her tie it around her back.

"Thanks," she says. "I hope this doesn't get you in trouble with those assholes." I look up and see Nader standing there, glaring at me. "Ronald's been looking for a reason to beat Nader's ass for months."

"I'd like to see that," I say.

She shakes her head no. "Whenever Ronald fights, there's blood. I hate blood."

Nader is still staring at me while I talk to Charlotte. Petra is trying to get the two other guards on duty to stop writing up Nader's violation on the report clipboard.

"Promise not to tell him?" Charlotte asks.

I've never talked to Ronald in my life. The guy is totally intimidating, not to mention twenty. "Yeah, okay."

Kim the pool manager arrives back from her lunch break, and after reading the clipboard report and talking to a few members, she kicks Nader out of the pool for the rest of the day, loudly. Jovially, even. They're friends because Nader works here and dates Petra, so Kim's really only doing it for show. She even towel-whips him on his way out the gate. Then he turns to me before he hops onto his bike, and says, "You're mine, Linderman!"

I hate that word: *Linderman*. No matter what I do, I can never get away from it. It's like we're cursed.

LUCKY LINDERMAN IS
UNDER STRICT ORDERS

My granny Janice Linderman died when I was seven. She had colon cancer. I remember the day clearly—I had a loose tooth that I was afraid to pull and two new Transformers in tow. I was playing in the corner of her living room, where she'd lived for the last month in a rented hospital bed alongside whatever hospice nurse was on duty, while Mom and Dad took turns talking softly to Granny Janice about how it was okay to die.

"Don't worry about us," Dad said in the softest voice I ever heard him use. I think he was crying.

"We'll take care of everything," Mom said, motioning me over to the bedside to say good-bye.

Granny Janice's final breaths smelled like week-old oysters. She was pretty high on morphine and talking to herself. I didn't know what to say, so I held her hand tightly and said, "Good-bye, Granny. I love you."

Her fluttering eyelids lurched open, and she grabbed my forearm so hard that it left a red mark that outlived her. She said, "Lucky, you have to rescue my Harry! He's still in the jungle being tortured by those damn gooks!"

"Gooks?" I asked.

"It's the medicine, Lucky," Mom whispered to me.

"You have to find him and bring him back! You need a father!" Granny blurted.

Then she died.

My mother sent me out of the room, which was fine by me, but she couldn't erase those words from my memory. If Granny Janice needed me to do something, then I'd do it, even if I didn't quite understand her orders.

Up until the cancer, Granny was my parent, I guess. When I was little, she'd watch me at her house while my parents worked. She'd sit at the kitchen table making phone calls and doing paperwork all day while I played with all of the cool old toys in her toy box. One time she told me that she wished I could live with her. I remember thinking that would be nice. Before she got cancer, the school bus would drop me at her door, and she would help me with my homework and feed me dinner until my mom would pick me up at six. It was just the way things were, and I liked it that way.

Dad's eyes were red, and he put his face in his hands. I picked up my Transformers and moved to the sunroom, and while Mom and Dad made the calls they had to make, I went straight to work.

I renamed Optimus Prime "Gook" and shifted an overgrown houseplant into the corner to make a jungle. I went to Granny Janice's toy box and dug out a small doll that had come with a farm set—a farmer in a hat, missing one leg after I'd bent it too far backward the previous Christmas—and I buried him to his waist in the houseplant soil and called him "Harry." While the coroner came and removed the body and helped my parents fill out paperwork, I rescued Harry from Gook about twenty times (by helicopter, riverboat, waterfall, ambush) before it was finally time to leave.

On our way home we stopped at a small neighborhood bar and grill and ate hamburgers in silence. Dad was just eating what he could, which wasn't much, and the only thing Mom could do was point out the train set that was suspended above the middle of the dining room, as if I were five. I swear, she nearly called it a *choo-choo*. I decided to go to the bathroom to escape.

I didn't really have to pee, but I went through the motions at the urinal anyway. About a minute after I got there, Nader McMillan came in and stood at the neighboring urinal. He was seven like me, but a lot taller (though that wouldn't be difficult). He peed like he'd been holding it in for a week. It splashed off the urinal and the little lemon-shaped disk at the bottom. I felt some splash-back hit my arm, but I didn't say anything because I knew Nader from first-grade recess and knew he was mean. I just stood there, little penis in hand, aiming but not peeing, praying he wouldn't notice me.

"What are you looking at?" he asked, even though my eyes hadn't moved. He turned toward me and peed on my sandals. On my feet. On my shins.

I didn't say anything and neither did he. He shook and zipped back up and didn't wash his hands before he left. I stood motionless, nervously wiggling my floppy tooth with my tongue until he was gone. Then I zipped myself and squished over to the sink. My feet felt disgusting, and I was debating whether to take off my sandals and wash them, when my dad and the manager came in. They looked at the pee puddle on the terracotta-tiled floor.

"Christ, Lucky," Dad said.

The manager said, "Doesn't look like an accident to me, man." He opened a small closet door to the right of the urinals and retrieved a mop, a bucket and a stand-up yellow plastic sign that read WET FLOOR.

"It wasn't me," I said. "It was that Nader kid."

Dad looked at the manager and said, "Really — he's a good kid."

"I'm sure he is. But Mr. McMillan is a regular patron here, and his kid said he saw your son doing it."

I shook my head and started to cry.

Five minutes later we were driving home, silent, with Styrofoam carriers on our laps. As we drove through Frederickstown toward our little suburban development, I watched the big houses on Main Street pass by and I twisted my loose tooth right out of my jaw. Looking back, I guess that was the day that changed everything.

JUNGLE DREAM # 1

I was walking alone on a path. I was in my Spider-Man pajamas and red Totes slippers. The jungle was loud with birdcalls and the *zeep-zeep-zeep-zeep* of insects. I looked down a lot, like a kid does in a big place. I focused on the bugs and the fallen leaves rather than looking up at the enormous canopy and the vines and the endlessness of it all.

When I came to a stream, I looked for rocks so I could cross it. I saw my red fleece slipper reach out for the first flat rock, and I saw it slide, and felt myself go off balance, until I was wet, bottom first, in the stream.

"Here, son," someone said in a hushed and husky voice. I looked up, and there was a skinny man with a bushy gray beard holding his hand out to me. "Come on. No sense crying. You'll be dry in no time."

I took his hand and he helped me cross to the other side. When I got there, he looked me up and down. "Those are very cool pajamas. I wish Frankie could get me a pair with Spider-Man on the front." He wore a pair of thinning black pajamas that stopped mid-shin, and was barefoot. His feet were a mess of sores and scars.

"Who are you?" I asked. "And who's Frankie?"

The man cocked his head to the side and studied me some more, stroked his beard with his right hand and smiled. "Don't you worry about that," he said. "Follow me and we'll dry those pajamas." He walked to a sparkling clearing of sun rays, and I followed, the water squishing through my toes in my Totes.

Halfway there, a mean-looking Asian man in a worn uniform jumped out of a thatched bamboo hut. He pointed a rifle at me and yelled, "Lindo-man, who the kid?"

• • •

I woke up instantly, still wet, and screaming. Mom was standing over me, shaking me awake. "It's just a bad dream," she said. "It's just a bad dream."

It was two in the morning. Mom was tiptoeing around because she didn't want to wake Dad, who had to get up in only a few hours to go to work at his new chef job. She said, handing me a pair of dry pajamas, "Just put these on. Don't worry. Accidents happen." I was still half inside the dream, hearing those final words that woke me. *Lindo-man, who the kid?*

Linderman.

Linderman.

It was Granddad. The man I was supposed to rescue. I'd found him.

RESCUE MISSION #1—A WEEK LATER

This time, as I walked toward the stream, I saw other things on the path. I saw little traps—holes dug with leaf cover to sprain an ankle in. Before I came to the clearing where the stream was, I found a group of spikes and poked them with a stick. I continued to push them until the square bit of wood lay on its side, revealing the six-inch-long nails that were hammered through it. I couldn't be sure, but there was something smeared all over the nails, and I think it was poop.

I crossed the stream without falling in and came to the bamboo huts outside the fenced-in area. The sounds of the jungle were deafening this time. Like when the cicadas come in Pennsylvania, except it wasn't familiar. It was all wild and scary.

"Psst."

I looked around but couldn't see who was making the noise.

"Kid! Look up!"

I looked up and there he was, the skinny man with the beard, sitting on a long branch of a tree. He was cross-legged, though it seemed physically impossible that he could sit that way on a tree branch, and he beckoned to me.

I eyed the trunk of the tree. There was no way I could get up. "How'd you get up there?" I asked.

"It's a dream, son. You can go anywhere you want."

So I closed my eyes and put myself in the tree next to him. We stared at each other. He sat up tall, his back straight, and smiled.

"Why are you up a tree?" I asked.

"Because it's better than *not* being up a tree."

"I saw the spikes," I said, thinking that's what he must have meant—that being up a tree was safer than being on the ground.

"The what?"

"The spikes. You know — the nails in the ground?"

He acknowledged what I meant. "Oh! Charlie's booby traps! Gotcha."

"Who's Charlie?"

He reached out and patted my hand. "Never you mind, son. It's nothing you need to worry about."

Somehow, right then I knew for sure this really was my grandfather. I looked at him and could see my dad's face in his face. I could see my face, too. It was a trustworthy face.

"Granddad?"

"Yeah?"

"What do I do about Nader McMillan?"

"Who's that?" he asked.

"The kid who peed on my feet. He's mean to everybody."

"A bully?"

"Yeah," I said. "A big one."

The old man thought for a minute. "Do you know what my mother told me to do to bullies?"

"No."

"She told me to ignore them. I think you should ignore that kid, too."

"But he peed on me."

He rubbed his chin through his beard. "He may have peed on your feet, but nobody can pee on your soul without your permission."

I had no idea what this meant.

"What if ignoring him doesn't work?"

"Then you get back to me. We'll figure it out together."

"Okay," I said, and glanced toward the camp below. I took note of the huts, some abandoned, some in use. "Is this a camp?" I asked.

"Yes. A prison camp."

My eyes moved to the barbed-wire fence surrounding a larger thatched hut. "Prison camp?"

He nodded.

"So you're a bad guy? A robber or something?"

He exhaled and let his straight back curve. "No, son. I'm not a bad guy."

I looked around the jungle and down at the prison camp. "So why are you here?"

He laughed as if he might be crazy or happy or something. When he was done, he said, "My number came up."

I shook my head.

"The lottery, Lucky. They picked my number and drafted me. A year later I was in Vietnam fighting in a war. A year after that I was a prisoner of war, and a year after that they started moving me around to places like this."

"Because of a number?" This did not mesh with my idea of a lottery. I'd watched those five-minute Powerball lottery shows with my mom. I was pretty sure nobody went to war because of the Ping-Pong balls with numbers on them.

"Yep. Number fourteen." He put a small green twig in his mouth and scraped each remaining tooth clean. "Each day of the year was assigned a number. March first, my birthday, was assigned number fourteen. Got it?"

I didn't get it. Not at all.

"Well, don't cry, son. There's nothing we can do about it now." He put his arm around me, and the two of us switched positions. We sat on the branch, hugging each other, our legs swinging, me sobbing into the old man's chest.

After a minute of this, Granny's voice came back to me, and I remembered why I was there. I wiped my tears on his shirt and looked him square in the eye.

"I'm getting you out of here, Granddad," I said. "I'm going to bring you home."

THE THIRD THING YOU NEED
TO KNOW — THE TURTLE

When we get home from the pool, I am still totally preoccupied by the Charlotte Dent bikini-top incident and the last thing Nader said to me. *You're mine, Linderman.* God, what a dick.

We walk in the back door and Dad is in the kitchen, stirring sugar into a pitcher of fresh iced tea and humming a Bruce Springsteen song.

"You want two or three ears of corn?" He asks this as if the whole scene is normal. Him here, cooking dinner, being my dad. Being *present.*

"Two, please."

I go into my room and change out of my pool stuff. I sit on my bed and think about Nader McMillan and wonder what I'm going to do. Ignore him. Stand up to him. Avoid him. Be "tough." I think of the stuff Dad has said over the years. How he finally gave up suggesting things. *Why are you asking me this? I never figured out what to do about my own bullies. How am I supposed to know what to do with yours?*

I tried all of his ideas. I even tried a few he never suggested. I tried sucking up to Nader and being his friend, which only worked for a little while during freshman year until I got him in trouble with the questionnaire. I tried talking to one of the guidance counselors last January, only to hear that Nader is a pain, yes, but the best thing to do is stay out of his way. "He's probably a good kid underneath it all," the counselor said. Which isn't true. But it meant Nader could keep treating kids like that, charming all the teachers with his perfect, whitened smile, and still play baseball in the spring. And it meant his lawsuit-happy lawyer father would stay off the school district's back.

"Lori, you ready to eat?" Dad yells.

She answers, "Two minutes!"

"Lucky! Do your business and wash your hands," he says. It's as if since my dad started working in Le Fancy-Schmancy Café, he thinks I stopped growing. I'm not seven anymore. I know when I need to pee.

When I sit at the table, they are both smiling at me and I frown. My father starts dishing out portions of barbecued honey-and-fresh-herb-marinated chicken and grilled, peppered corn on the cob. He points to the bowl of buttery, parsley-sprinkled new potatoes on the table and says, "Help yourself."

This is a normal meal, considering it's usually lightly

seared chicken medallions glazed with blackberry sauce or stuffed with foie gras, or pork chops breaded with organic mushroom dust and served with *petits pois* peas smothered in garlic and almond butter, with a dash of lime. I don't know where he gets this from. Granny Janice was fond of Spam, macaroni and cheese out of a box and grilled cheese sandwiches.

While I'm halfway through my second ear of corn, Mom says, "Lucky helped a girl at the pool today. It was very sweet."

Dad looks at me and nods his head. "Proud of you."

"Do you want to tell him what else happened?" Mom asks.

"Nah." I'm not even sure what she's talking about, but I think it's Nader being an asshole. How is this news?

"What happened?" he asks.

"It was nothing," I say, diving back into my ear of corn.

"He got pushed around by that McMillan boy again," she says.

"I perfected the cannonball, too. You should see it," I say.

"Did you push him back?"

I pretend we're not talking about this. "Huh?"

Mom says, "The McMillan boy. He wants to know if you pushed back."

"No."

"Good. Fighting is for sissies," he says.

I wish I could tell him how much I disagree.

I wish he would fight himself and win me.

But that's the thing, isn't it? The thing about my dad?

There's no point in disagreeing with him because he already does it all by himself. Here's an example.

Have you ever seen those POW/MIA flags? The black ones with the soldier and the guard tower, with the words YOU ARE NOT FORGOTTEN across the bottom, like this?

We have them plastered all over our cars, our windows, our stuff—my baseball bat and Mom's bird feeders. We have a flagpole in the front yard where we fly the biggest POW/ MIA flag that will fit. My father sews a patch on my winter coat every year. And my swimming trunks. And my gym uniform. I have exactly fourteen different POW/MIA T-shirts. He has it tattooed on his right arm, has a license plate holder, a set of coasters, mugs and playing cards.

In our house the slogan rings true. There is no way to forget our missing heroes here. No way. But we never really talk about it.

And then he says, "Fighting is for sissies."

Some days I want to tie the two of them to the sofa and speak my mind. Say stuff. Real stuff. Ask stuff. *How come we gave up on Granddad when Granny Janice died? Why did she ask me to rescue him? Why didn't she ask you? And why aren't we doing something? Anything?*

The only *real* thing I ever heard Dad say was, "It would have been better if my dad had come home in a bag, because then at least we would know." Then he transforms into a turtle.

Of course, the shell is the biggest part of a turtle.

And we never really talk about it.

5

OPERATION DON'T SMILE EVER—
FRESHMAN YEAR

The day after Evelyn Schwartz went blabbing to the guidance office about my suicide survey, Danny and Nader got a lecture from the principal. I know this because Danny told me on the bus home from school.

"Why'd you have to ruin our joke?"

"I didn't think it was a big deal," I said.

"Fish says he's going to call my dad, man." We called the principal, Mr. Temms, "Fish" because his eyes bulged and his head was flat.

"Why?"

"You know why. They're all retards, that's why."

"Huh," I said.

"And Nader is *pissed*," he added.

"Him too?"

"We got called down together," he said. "To check out your stupid little story."

"Shit."

"Yeah, shit. Nader's dad will flip out, too."

"I'm really sorry," I said. "I didn't think it was that big of a deal."

"Once Nader finds you, you'll be way sorrier."

"You think?"

"The guy's a maniac."

"Yeah, but we're — kind of friends now, aren't we?"

He laughed and shook his head. "Not anymore, you're not."

I tried to look like I didn't give a shit. "Whatever. I'm in enough trouble as it is. My parents got called into a meeting next week. They're going to test me or something."

"What? Test if you're an idiot?"

I nudged him on the arm. "Yeah, right?"

"Because I can tell them that," he said.

The meeting was on a Tuesday. But Nader found me on Monday, in the locker room after gym.

"Hey, Linderman! Pay attention!" he shouted.

Then he grabbed the shortest, scrawniest kid in the locker room and threw him into the corner bench. He had his friends hold him down, take off his clothes, and blindfold him with his smelly gym uniform. The more the kid screamed and kicked, the more of Nader's minions helped to hold him down, legs open. I could see him struggling against their hands, trying to bring his knees together. I could see him shaking. Breathing heavily. Panicking. Gagging.

While the other boys chanted "Don't barf, pussy!" Nader produced a banana from his gym locker, walked over to the toilets, dipped it, and said, "Watch closely, Linderman, because this is what snitches get."

That night I made my first booby trap.

RESCUE MISSION #49 — BOOBY TRAP

I was in a pit, up to my knees in water. It was raining frogs. Big, fat green raindrops with legs that hopped the minute they landed. They were in my shorts. In my shirt. They were in my brain. There were leeches sucking life out of my ankles and calves. The frogs were trying to gnaw them off with their sharp frog teeth. It was agony.

This was my forty-ninth mission to rescue Granddad, so it wasn't the first time I'd seen frog rain, leeches or the jungle. So far we'd never quite made it all the way out. Obviously.

On our many journeys together, Granddad had showed me how to make booby traps, but I'd never done it by myself before. I took my machete to the bamboo and whittled it into spikes. A hundred spikes. No one could see me because the pit was a mile off the jungle path and hidden by underbrush that was impossible to get through.

Granddad was sleeping ten feet away. I'd helped him escape Frankie's prison camp the night before, and we'd been hacking through the vast jungle all day. I stayed in the pit through the night, carving spikes until they were sharp enough to cut stone. I tested one on my left index finger, and I barely had to connect to draw blood. I set them into the trap and covered the hole around me.

Then I was so tired I fell asleep standing up, my head resting on the muddy side of the frog-drenched pit, still knee-deep in leeches.

Granddad Harry woke me up inside the dream.

"You ready?"

He pulled me out and set me on the side of the hole. There were so many leeches, I thought I'd rather amputate my legs than pull each one off. The rain had stopped, but not for long. The sky was still cloudy, and this break was the cruel joke of the rainy season—a moment to pretend you weren't soaked to the marrow and being eaten alive by the jungle.

Granddad dragged me to the shelter he'd made out of a tarp and three bamboo poles. I said, "I need to cover the pit. Finish the job."

He thought I was delirious, and I probably was. My legs were just blood and bites and animals and teeth. I passed out by the time he got to the fourth leech. There were at least one hundred to go.

When I came to, curled under the tarp, it was raining frogs again. I looked over to my booby trap and it was perfect. My legs ached as if they were shot with salt pellets. Even the bones hurt. When I looked down, and my eyes adjusted to the dim monsoon light, I saw that my legs looked as if they'd been attacked by a tiger.

Granddad said, "You need to heal those legs, son."

"Ughhhh." This was supposed to be me speaking, but I couldn't speak. I drooled out this sound.

"Go back to sleep. I'll try to get us to a hospital."

I knew he was lying. How could an escaped POW from the Vietnam War walk into a hospital with his wounded half-dream grandson and get help? It was impossible. I was going to die there.

If I was going to die, then I wanted to die with honor. I'd rescued my long-missing grandfather, and I wanted him to get out the rest of the way without me.

I said, "Iiihyyyyy."

If I was going to die, then I wanted to die without secrets. I tried to tell Granddad about the banana incident and what Nader did to snitches.

I said, "Ttrroooooo."

Nothing came out right. The leeches ate my brain. They ate my tongue.

Granddad Harry stroked my head and handed me a cigar. "Congratulations on your first booby trap, son. Now go back home and get yourself some rest."

• • •

When I woke up, out of breath and completely freaked out, I tried to calm myself with the words Mom always said when I'd woken up from jungle dreams before: "It was just a bad dream, Lucky. Just a bad dream."

But it wasn't just a dream. I still had the cigar in my hand.

LUCKY LINDERMAN HIDES
THINGS UNDER HIS BED

Last night after dinner and his "Fighting is for sissies" declaration, Dad showed up at my bedroom door.

"Help me take down the flag?" he said.

I followed him to the front lawn, where we took down the POW/MIA flag, followed by the American flag. Usually he does this by himself, so it was nice helping him fold them into perfect triangles.

After that he went back to work and I went into my room and read my book. It's called *One Shot, One Kill,* and it's about snipers in different American wars. Lara Jones never fails to tell me that my reading about war makes me weird, but I can't get her fascination with reading about fairies and wizards, so I guess that makes us even.

After the dreams started to come every other month or

so — when I about was nine — I started reading about the war as much as I could. My elementary school library had a set of World Book encyclopedias and I pulled out the U–V volume one day and found "The Vietnam War" on page 372 and read about it, even though I had no real idea of what it was talking about. All sorts of names and places I'd never heard of (*Gulf of Tonkin, Laos, Cambodia, Vietcong, Indochina, Ho Chi Minh*). Dates (*1957, 1964, 1973, 1975*). Numbers (*approximately 9,000,000 US military served; 58,000 dead; 300,000 wounded; 2,300 missing at the end of the war*). And there were three pictures: one of a helicopter hovering inches above a clearing in the jungle, and three soldiers providing cover; one of protesters at the Capitol in Washington, DC; and one of a bunch of Vietnamese people stuffed into a helicopter during the evacuation of Saigon in 1975.

Every time I went to the library, I revisited page 372 to see if I could understand more. This went on through middle school, when I started to read other Vietnam-related books, too. I figured out who "Charlie" was — that it was just a nickname for the enemy, the Vietcong, or the VC: the Communist soldiers fighting for North Vietnam to take over our allies in South Vietnam.

Then, when I was twelve, I took a trip to the attic to find an old baseball mitt, and I discovered the box — the box from Granny Janice's house filled with keepsakes and paperwork and books and letters about Granddad Harry's case. Even though it was a hot, late-spring day and the attic was sweltering, I went through the whole box, paper by paper. That's where I found *One Shot, One Kill*. It's where I found all the letters between Granny Janice and the government. It's where I found out she was a big-time member of the POW/MIA movement who spoke at rallies and national meetings and worked with the families of the missing. There were newspaper clippings, including a big one about how the government decided to classify all missing as "presumed dead" and how Granny Janice refused to see it that way.

It quoted her. "No one has proved to me that my husband isn't still alive somewhere in Southeast Asia. So, as far as I'm concerned, if even one man is alive, we owe him more than this—than presuming him dead for the sake of tidying paperwork."

There were more than twenty clippings, from places all over the country where she was invited to speak. Some had pictures. There was even a picture of her at the White House. This made me realize that Granny was a hero as much as Granddad was.

At the bottom of the box, I found a shoe box full of love letters between her and Granddad Harry from the time he was in training all the way up to when he was captured. I took it and hid it under my bed at the bottom of an old box of Transformers.

There's this one letter I read nearly every day.

Dear Janice,
   I'm sorry it's been so long since I wrote. Back in August they plucked me right out of my platoon and

sent me for training in the mountains over by Long Binh. I'm now a US Army sniper.

Last week I sat in a tree for over twenty-four hours watching a VC spy with his family in a village. When I dropped him, I watched his wife and kids throw themselves on his dead body. Janice, God knows if anyone did it to you, I'd find them in hell and make them wish they didn't. When I killed deer with my father, it never felt like this.

But I don't want you to know these things. You are a beautiful woman who deserves to hear beautiful things. This will make you laugh: They gave me a nickname. Because I'm so good at my job (a confirmed twenty kills) the enemy has a price on my head, but so far Charlie can't catch me. So my PL named me Lucky. Lucky Linderman. Has a ring to it, don't you think?

Sometimes I dream of you and your skin. The way you smell. And I know that this will all be over soon and we can make perfect love with each other again. The boys on the front had magazines with pinups, and they talked about how one day they would score women like that, but they're kids. They don't know what love is. Here they learn what hate is, and I am so sad that they might never know love because hate came first. Maybe they will miss out on having a woman like you, and I feel sorry for them.

I can't wait to be a great father to Victor and an outstanding husband to you. Janice, you deserve it.

Since that day I saw you in chemistry class with that canary yellow skirt, I wanted to make every day Christmas for you. I know waiting for me must be hard. Please remember how much I love you.

All my love,
Harry

This letter was the last personal letter Granny Janice received. Then, he was gone.

No one could explain it. In the box in the attic, we have a ton of letters from the government that asked to change Harry's status to "presumed dead." But they never had proof. No bones or tags or anything. No one ever returned his wedding ring or his teeth. In the end, they changed the status without her permission, but it's a lie.

The last she ever heard, he might have been alive in a Lao prison camp in 1987, fourteen years after the end of the war. This information came from fifteen unrelated sources — mostly refugees and boat people, and only thanks to the civilian POW/MIA organization that Granny Janice had worked for. The Pathet Lao (Communist Laos) returned very few US prisoners after the Vietnam War.

Under a dozen.

This was okay because we didn't technically have a war with Laos. This was okay because our government wanted to move the nation into a more positive political era. This was not okay with the more than six hundred families who'd lost track of their loved ones in Laos.

Of course, it was easy to assume that these men who never returned from the war had died from jungle diseases. Jungle diseases suck. There's dysentery, which goes like this: constant bloody diarrhea until you die. And malaria, which goes something like this: fever, body aches, vomiting and convulsions until you die. Also beriberi, which sounds way fruitier than this: weight loss, body pain, going crazy, swelling limbs, paralysis and heart abnormalities until you die.

It was also easy to assume that these missing men had died from an assortment of war wounds — from stinging shrapnel to torture injuries to booby-trap infections, thanks to the practice of coating spikes in a variety of infectious materials. But some men survive all sorts of crazy stuff, and Communists at the time were known for holding live prisoners for use as political currency or a ticket out of their unstable country.

So every time the government tried to make Granny Janice sign a piece of paper declaring Harry dead, she fought it. I can see her saying, "Up yours! My Harry is not dead!" Because Granny Janice figured Harry could survive anything to see her one last time.

Of course, now I know it, too.

RESCUE MISSION #101 — PLAYING GIN WITH FRANKIE

Granddad, his guard Frankie and I are playing a game of gin under the canopy of the jungle. I'm winning. Granddad is not really paying attention, because he is too busy swatting red ants off his ankles. He's missing three fingers on his left hand.

"Aren't you guys getting eaten alive out here?"

I look down at my ankles. No ants. "Nope."

Frankie ignores us and is concentrating hard on his cards.

Granddad gets up and sees that his chair is right on top of an anthill, so he moves to another part of the card table, and play continues.

Frankie turns to me and says, "How you dealing with that jerk in school, Lucky Lindo-man?"

I shrug. "It's under control," I say. I hadn't talked about Nader with Granddad for years. How could I complain about titty twisters at recess to a guy who was missing his limbs or his teeth or his whole damn life? I know he told me to come to him if ignoring Nader didn't work, and I wanted to, but I'd stopped telling any adults about it in real life, and here in the jungle it felt too whiny.

And I wasn't there to whine. I was there to outsmart Frankie, kill him if I had to, and then rescue Granddad Harry.

"Gin!" I say, and I lay down my run of diamonds and four queens.

Frankie picks up his rifle and puts it to my head. "Why don't you tell us the truth, kid?"

Granddad is standing now. "Frankie, put the gun down."

"But he don't tell you the truth, Harry. He lie."

I duck, punch Frankie in the gut and grab his rifle from him. I kick him to the ground and put my bare foot on his neck. Granddad sits on his torso. I put the rifle to his head.

"It's none of your goddamn business how my life is," I say. "You got that?"

He nods quickly. My finger jitters on the trigger.

"Don't kill me! Please!" he says.

I laugh. But my trigger finger just won't pull.

Granddad says, "Don't, Lucky."

"I'm getting you out of here, Granddad. For good. Forever."

"I let you go," Frankie says. "You go and I never see you again!"

I kick him in the face. His nose bleeds instantly.

"Lucky, stop," Granddad says.

"Why are you defending him? He's tortured you for your whole life!"

"He's fed me, too."

I look at Granddad and figure he must be suffering from some freaky kind of Stockholm syndrome, where you bond with a kidnapper.

"He brainwashed your ass," I say. I point the rifle right at Frankie's temple. "I'm taking you home."

When I feel my finger pull the trigger, I wake up.

• • •

Next to me on my pillow is a winning hand of gin. An ace, two, three, four, five and six of diamonds and four queens. The cards are coated in four decades' worth of jungle dirt.

I pull out my Transformers box from under my bed and put the cards in, alongside all my other jungle souvenirs that

I'd collected over the years: the very first one — a small rusty bolt I'd found when I was ten, the cigar from my first booby trap, a small block of wood with nails hammered through it. A petrified frog. Two rocks. A map. An empty C ration can. An assortment of metal parts.

I lie back down for a while, feeling like a jungle hero. But then I hear Mom and Dad talking in the living room, and I remember that I am a weak suburban failure.

LUCKY LINDERMAN IS *NOT* MAKING SCRAMBLED EGGS

Le Smugasbord is closed on Mondays, so we treat Mondays in the summertime the way most people treat Sunday. Dad is required to stick around all day if possible, though he usually only makes it until midafternoon before something we do makes him mad. Around ten, Mom comes to my bedroom door and says, "Lucky? You want some brunch?"

I groan and tell her I'll be there in ten minutes.

Through my one half-open eye, I see her put a pair of swimming trunks on my dresser. "I bought these a size too big last year. I think they'll fit you now."

When I arrive in the kitchen, I realize I've been set up. The eggs are still in the carton next to an empty bowl. The whisk is sitting on the counter next to the bowl. There's a loaf of bread by the fridge, and an empty frying pan on the stove.

Oh, God. Not this again — the once-a-month attempt to give-a-shit-through-cooking.

Before I can turn around and go back to my room, Dad arrives next to me, and Mom is at the kitchen doorway.

"French toast or scrambled eggs? It's up to you," he says.

"I don't care. Whatever you guys want," I say.

"Nope," Mom says. "It's your choice!"

I go to the cabinet with the cereal in it and pull out a box of Cheerios. I grab a bowl and am about to get a spoon out of the drawer, but Dad stops me.

"Come on, man. Just for fun. Let's make breakfast together."

"Why?" I ask.

"Why not? How come you don't want to cook with your old man anymore?"

"Dunno. Just don't think I'm good at it," I say.

"You were great at it once. Aren't you the only person in the family who can crack an egg and not get shell?"

"I doubt I could do that anymore."

"These things take practice. Remember when we used to make pancakes and waffles together?"

I was seven. That makes it over half my life ago. I don't tell him this.

"I'm fine with cereal. I'm not really that hungry."

"I don't think that's the real reason," Dad says.

I'm too tired and cranky to deal with this. So, I decide if Dad wants to talk about *real reasons*, then I will. I put the box of Cheerios on the table and look him square in the eye.

"I don't want to talk about food anymore. It's all you ever

talk about. I don't want to cook with you, and I don't want to watch the stupid Food Channel with you, either," I say.

He stands there and just stares at me.

Mom says, "Your father talks about more than food." Defector.

He mutters under his breath like we can't hear it. He says something about how nothing he does is ever good enough.

"No, because if you tried, then it would be good enough," I say. "But you don't."

He looks at Mom and she shrugs. She lowers her head as though she might agree with me. She's a crazy double agent.

"I guess I'm not needed here," he says, and goes to get his keys off the counter.

"Actually, Dad, that's the problem. You *are* needed here. I *do* need a father, you know?"

He slams the keys onto the counter. "God*damn* it! You don't have any idea what it's like not having a father! You don't know how good you have it!"

He walks straight through the front door and to his car, gets in, backs down the driveway and takes off.

My mother sighs. A big one. Then she sits down at the kitchen table and sighs again. Another big one. She rubs her forehead with her fingertips until she can figure out what to say.

Then she gets up, puts the whisk back in the drawer and says, "Why couldn't you just have fun and cook some eggs? He needs that."

"Well, I needed stuff, too, but when I needed it, he wasn't here, was he?" I say. "I gave up trying after my thirteenth birthday. Remember that?"

The week I turned thirteen, I was so sick of Dad only caring about food that I swore off eating until my mother took me to the doctor. I think I lasted six days. The doctor examined me and asked me a bunch of gastronomical questions — mostly about poop and any pains I might have.

"You seem fine," he said.

"I am fine."

He looked at Mom, who was sitting on the chair next to the exam table. "Lori, do you mind giving us a minute?"

She left, and he turned back to me. "Do you want to tell me what's really going on?"

"I hate my father," I said.

"Why?"

"He works all the time and doesn't care about us." I added, "He hardly talks to us."

"My father rarely talked to me, either," he said. "But I didn't stop eating because of it."

"What did you do?"

His tone changed. "I grew up and realized how silly I was being."

On the way home I asked Mom, "Do you ever think that if you were a pork chop or a leg of lamb, Dad would pay more attention to you?"

She laughed. "Yes, Lucky. I have felt that way."

"What did you do about it?"

"I don't know," she answered. But I knew. She swam more laps.

THE FOURTH THING YOU NEED
TO KNOW—THE ANTS

The Freddy pool is looking especially inviting today. Mom comments to Kim the manager about her stellar water quality. Kim mentions something about calcium levels. It's very exciting stuff here on a sunny Tuesday in July. Seriously. Could we all be more boring?

I head into the bathroom to change and am happy to find that the new swim shorts Mom gave me aren't those annoying extra-large puffy things. These are a little gay, but at least they won't hang down and almost show my butt crack when I climb up the ladder, and I'm pretty sure they'll make for better cannonballs.

When I walk out of the men's room, Nader ambushes me.

He pulls and twists my arm so hard I think he's going to dislocate my shoulder. He pushes me onto the concrete and puts his knee in the middle of my back, the way the cops on TV do. He turns my face to the side and presses my cheek into the baking cement. I can feel it burn my skin.

Up close, I see the sparkling bits. I can see the tiny world ants see. Hills and valleys of concrete—crumbs from the snack bar, and the trail of water that leaks from the pipe under the water fountain between the bathrooms.

Nader begins to move my face across it—slowly scraping me against sandpaper. He says, "See what happens when you fuck with me, Linderman?"

I don't say anything. My face stings and I tense it. He drags it more, pressing it so hard I swear my cheekbone is going to shatter. I can feel the skin melting off it. I feel oddly happy. Peaceful. Like I'm going crazy.

Ants appear on the concrete in front of me. Dancing ants. Smiling ants. Ants having a party. One tells me to hang on. *Don't worry, kid!* he says, holding up a martini glass. *It'll be over in a minute!*

"Answer me!" Nader says.

Time has slowed to a complete head-fuck. I can't say anything. I don't think he knows how hard he's pressing my face into the concrete. And yet the smell of the concrete is pleasant. The ants continue dancing.

Danny pokes his head around the wall.

Nader says, "See what happens when you fuck with me, dude?"

Danny says, "Come on, man. He's all right."

"Answer me!" Nader says again.

I don't know what to say, so I say, "What did I do?"

He laughs. "You fucked with me. Remember? Helping that little slut? See what happens? Karma, dude! Say it! Bad shit happens!" He jerks my face with every enunciation.

I concentrate on the feeling of my skin peeling off my cheek. I wonder will the ants eat it after this is over. Do ants eat skin?

"Say it, Linderman! Bad. Shit. Happens."

I say, "Bad shit happens."

"Now keep your fucking mouth shut," he says into my ear. He's so close I can smell the toothpaste he used this morning.

He gets up and struts behind the bathhouse to his bike and rides off.

While I lie there for a second or two, I have one of my old Transformers daydreams from when I was seven. I am Optimus Prime, and I grow to the size of the entire swimming pool. I stomp Nader into dust. I regrow him like dehydrated potatoes, and then I stick him in my prison camp. There are a lot of bamboo spikes. I make him eat rat shit. The ants all laugh.

I'm sitting up, propped against the men's room doorjamb, and Kim the pool manager is squinting at my face.

"Jesus, Lucky!"

I blink.

"You okay?"

I nod feebly. At the same time I hold back maniacal laughter, suppressing my inner crazy person who is still watching ants dance. One of them is popping the cork on a bottle of champagne. Another is setting up a limbo stick.

"Who did it?" she asks, looking around. I glance at Danny, who's now in place behind the snack-bar counter with his head through the window, craning his neck so he can see us.

She says, "Who did this to him?"

He shrugs. Asshole.

"Come on. I have to clean that," she says, and helps me up. She signals to the guard on duty to get Mom's attention. I reach up and touch my right cheek. It's sticky and bloody, and it hurts like the road rash I got when I crashed my bike when I was eight.

"Brace yourself. It's just water, okay?" She holds a bottle of distilled water the way I hold mustard when I'm about to squirt it onto a hot dog, and she cleanses the wound — which is my entire cheek. Mom arrives at the door of the office with a towel wrapped around her.

"Lucky? What happened?"

"I — uh — got — uh —" I can't finish the sentence, because she wraps her arm around my shoulder and looks closely at the damage. Her expression is a mix of intense concern and anger. Even though she's being soft to me, I can see her inner squid inking all over the place.

"He won't tell me who did it," Kim the manager says.

"We're going home." Mom turns and storms toward our stuff.

Kim the manager squats and looks at me as she applies Neosporin. "It's gonna heal better if I don't cover it." A nod at this, and she puts her hand on my arm. I've known her my whole life. She's put Band-Aids on my stubbed toes and treated the bee stings on the soles of my feet. She says, "You have to tell me who did this so I can boot 'em from the pool, buddy."

All I can think about is how they held that poor kid down in the locker room. How they all laughed.

I stare into her eyes as seriously as I can. "Nader," I whisper.

She looks at me skeptically. "McMillan? He's not even here yet," she says. She pokes her head out to inspect the empty bike rack where Nader usually parks his bike.

"Danny saw the whole thing," I say. "Ask him."

"Why would he do this?"

"He said it was karma," I say.

"That little jerk wouldn't know karma if it bit him on the nose," she says, trying to get me to laugh, but I don't.

She explains that she's stuck in the middle. She knows she should fire Nader, but if she does, she'll lose a guard, and guards are hard to come by in July.

The ants say: *Blah blah blah blah blah.*

I see Mom gesturing to herself in the distance. She mutters all the way to the blanket, gathers up our stuff and then aims herself back toward the office. When she gets back to where I'm sitting, watching the ants limbo, Kim is writing up a report on the clipboard. She and Mom have a talk about what happened, and they decide to let the pool board of directors deal with it because Kim promises "disciplinary action."

When we're leaving, Mom throws the bags into the trunk

so roughly, all the stuff comes out of them. She puts a towel on the driver's seat and actually burns rubber when she pulls out of the parking lot.

I've never seen her like this before.

At the intersection where she should take a left, she takes a right. She drives all the way to the big mall twenty minutes away and parks in the parking lot, leaves the car on for the AC and turns to me, in the backseat.

"Stay here. I'll be back in a minute."

She pops the trunk and finds her sundress and slips it on over her swimsuit. Then she gets her cell phone from her purse, leans against the bumper and dials a number. I hear her, and I know she's talking to Dad. I can't catch every word, but I hear her say, "Well, you were *wrong!*" She looks in at me, and I avoid eye contact.

The last thing I hear as she walks toward the double doors to the mall is "I can't take it anymore!"

All I want to do is run away. I just want to start over. I do not want to explain this to Dad. I feel like a failure. A loser. Another Linderman casualty. All I want to do is go to sleep and find Granddad Harry and stay there with him forever.

RESCUE MISSION #102 — BOOBY-TRAP THE POOL

I am in the pit again, but it is not raining frogs. It is not raining anything at all. It is nighttime, and there is no moon. The pit is dry, and the air is hot and dry. I have my stakes and a bowie knife. I have a pair of latex gloves. I have a plastic Tupperware container with the easy-pop lid in place. Inside the container is something brown.

I set each stake into the dirt, and hammer the points to get them in solid. I then resharpen the points with the knife, one by one, until all twenty of my stakes are there, pointing up — a bed of nails for a giant.

I stop and look around for Granddad Harry, and I see that I'm not in the jungle. I am at the Freddy pool, next to the bathroom doors at the edge of the chain-link fence. I'm in the secret smoking spot where Ronald and the other nicotine addicts go to get their fix. The ants are there. They are smoking cigarettes and have pointed party hats on their heads. I don't want to be here. I want to be with Granddad. In the jungle.

"Granddad!" I whisper-yell. "Psst!"

No one answers. The ants ignore me, too.

I adjust my eyes to the dark night and see familiar pool things: the diving board, the slide and the big oak tree. I look down at my body. I am the muscular dream-me, which is a relief. If I can't escape the Freddy pool, at least I can escape the real me at the Freddy pool. I decide to take a night swim. I decide to start with a perfect front flip, which I have never achieved in real life. I go to the board and bounce several times and do a perfect one-and-a-half.

In the pool, under the water, I feel I *belong* here. Like this is *my* pool. I do a lap of freestyle and a few laps of breaststroke. I figure since I'm in a dream and I just did a one-and-a-half, I might as well try the butterfly, too. I do a butterfly lap that would make Mom proud.

When I get into the shallow end and I stop to catch my breath, there is applause. It's Granddad. He's missing his left leg this time. This makes me remember that I am at war. I reach up to my cheek and I feel my own wound, sticky and fresh, and hop out of the pool, dry myself and make my way back to the pit. This booby trap is definitely not part of the primary objective, but this is guerilla shit now. Fuck the rules. Fuck the strategy. Fuck the rescue. Nader must die.

Granddad points to the pit. "You planning to trap someone?"

I nod.

"You know that probably won't go down well around here, right?" When he says that, he's wrestling with a rotten tooth, and he rips it right out of his gums and tosses it over the fence and into the road.

I say, "I'm just doing my job." Then I walk over to the roll of thin sod I've prepared to cover the hole and I drag it into place.

At this, Granddad disappears. I face the Tupperware container and the pit. As I slip into it for the last time, I think of Granddad's reasoning. This is a dream, right? I'm not really at the pool making a booby trap for Nader to fall into and die, am I? Did Granddad disappear because he's ashamed of me?

I put on the gloves and grab the Tupperware container. I pop the lid off, and the smell is awful. I retch. I smear a little bit onto every spike and then toss the container and the gloves to the bottom of the pit. I get out and roll the sod over the top, carefully smoothing it over the hole. I tell the ants in the grass to run or else they'll drown. They go back to smoking on the concrete. I take the hose that they use to fill the baby pool and spray down the sod so it doesn't dry out and look wrong.

As I walk home in the dark, I can see Granddad hopping on his remaining leg about a hundred yards in front of me, but I can't reach him no matter how fast I run.

• • •

"Lucky?"

It's Mom. She's waking me up. We're home.

"It's too hot to sleep in the car. Come on. Come inside."

When she gets out, I stay in the backseat for a minute. My hair is still wet from my dream swim. My hands smell of latex. I sit up and look at my face in the rearview mirror, and I wince when I see it.

When I get inside, Dad doesn't say anything about it. He doesn't look at me, either, when Mom waves a packet of paper at him. Airplane tickets. "We're going to Tempe for a few weeks. We're going to get Lucky away from this kid, and while we're gone you're going to do something about it."

I say, "Tempe? Arizona? In July? Can't we just stay here?"

"I didn't just pick the idea out of thin air," Mom says. "I want to see my brother and get out of here for a while. Plus, I think it'll do you some good." She means that we don't know any other people who have a pool in their backyard for her squid to swim in.

"I think it'll do you both some good," Dad says.

She shoots him a look that makes him focus on the floor and shut up. This isn't just about me. Or Nader. Or her wanting to see her brother. This is about them...only I'm getting blamed for it.

"I know it's a little last minute, but it's happening, so let's pack," she says to me.

Dad sighs.

I sigh.

She sighs.

The ants sigh.

I offer the most positive thing I can say, even though I frown while I say it. "This could be good, I guess. I've always wanted to get to know Uncle Dave."

PART TWO

An agreeable companion on a
journey is as good as a carriage.
—*Publilius Syrus*

THE FIFTH THING YOU NEED TO KNOW—THIS IS GOING TO SUCK

Mom and I arrive at the Phoenix Sky Harbor airport, and she won't let me on the moving sidewalks. "No point in rushing. Our bag won't be ready yet, anyway," she says. We brought one case of clothing because we only have one suitcase and didn't have time to buy another one before we left. Mom put a big X on it in yellow tape so we'd know it was ours when we got here.

Once we find our luggage-collection point, Mom puts me in prime grabbing territory and keeps an eagle eye on the rotating luggage. We watch as suitcase after suitcase arrives, and don't say anything. Mom looks tired.

"Lori! Lori! Lori!"

The voice sounds like a bird that got hit by a truck. Squawking. Insufferable. Mom winces a little.

"Jodi! Hey!"

They hug. Aunt Jodi nods at me. Her double chin multiplies when she does this. I nod back. I'm frowning, as usual—plus it's pretty hard to move your face when you're building a scab the size of a pancake on your cheek. Aunt Jodi scowls at my scab as though I brought it to annoy her. She doesn't say, "Nice to meet you," the way most people would when meeting someone—like a nephew they never met before.

"That's it," Mom says, squinting and pointing to a suitcase with a yellow *X*. (The yellow *X* which is completely unnecessary, considering our suitcase is from 1985 and luggage has come a long way since then.)

"You only brought one bag?" Jodi asks as I lug it off the conveyor. "God, when Dave and I went to Mexico last year, I took one bag just for my shoes!"

"I'm not a shoe person," Mom answers, monotone.

"Well, yeah. That's obvious."

Mom is wearing the only pair of sandals she owns. A pair of black Birkenstocks with rusty buckles. I'm suddenly especially proud of her for not being a shoe person.

Aunt Jodi is staring at my scab. I know this because I can feel her staring at it, even though I'm not looking at her. She whispers to Mom, "Is he okay? He looks awful!"

Mom blows her off—a sign that she's already mentally in Jodi's backyard pool doing laps.

When we walk out of the airport, it's as if we have walked into a pizza oven. I feel like a pie, baking. It's insane. I can't even sweat. My eyeballs are hot and dry. My lips become chapped before we even get to the parking lot. My scab puckers.

Once we're in the car with the air-conditioning blasting, Aunt Jodi talks annoyingly about tourist attractions, as if this is the reason we're here, when we all know it isn't. Halfway to the house she turns on news radio and shuts up. When we get there, Uncle Dave hugs me and then holds me at arm's length and gives my scab an evil look.

I only met Dave once before, three years ago. He and Mom are only siblings, and they look alike — same hair and cheekbones. He came to see us while he was in Harrisburg on business for a week, but I was twelve and stayed in my room a lot. Now he's saying, "Can't wait to show you my weight room," and "You watch baseball?" These comments make me confident that the next three weeks might not suck nearly as much as I thought they would back at the airport. At least we're not talking about bullshit like how beautiful desert sunsets are or the plethora of tourist attractions that the scabbed pronoun in the backseat would love.

After brief welcomes, Aunt Jodi shows us around. It's a one-story house with a long hallway back to Jodi and Dave's bedroom. The room across the hall is filled with various hobby items — a sewing machine, a treadmill, a scrapbooking table and Jodi's home computer, which is so old it must have two megs of RAM, tops. The floor is crammed with stacks of magazines. Mostly tabloids, like *People* and *Us*. Our room — the guest room, with two twin beds, a dresser and its own bathroom — is right off the living room/kitchen area.

"Please don't move any of the furniture," Jodi says. "It's all in the right place to move positive energy around the house. If there's anything you two need right now, it's positive energy, right?" She says this like a kindergarten teacher. As if her feeble attempt at feng shui will rebuild our family, cure my dad's turtle-itis and maybe even heal my scab. Mom excuses herself and goes into the guest bathroom.

I heave the suitcase onto Mom's bed and stare at Aunt Jodi until she gets the message. "I'll give you some space," she mutters, and waddles into the hallway. I close the door gently behind her and flop onto my bed.

Mom emerges from the bathroom with her swimsuit on and her towel draped over her right arm. While she swims and talks to Aunt Jodi, who sits on the side of the pool dangling her feet in the water, I turn on the TV in the living room and check to see whether Jodi and Dave get the Food Channel, but they don't. I go back to my bed and take a short nap, careful not to turn onto my right side so I don't stick to the pillowcase.

Can I call it a nap if I don't really sleep? Can I call it a nap if all I do is lie here and listen to the ants in my head saying things like: *Dude, this place sucks. You're perfectly matched. Maybe you should move here. We could rename it the Pussy State just for you.*

It's hard to believe that technically, only a few hours ago, I was getting my ass kicked by Nader McMillan outside the men's room at the Freddy pool. After a while, I get up and inspect my scab in the guest room mirror for the first time. It's dried into a sore, ugly, rucked-up plateau. Parts are cut more deeply than others. I swear he nearly revealed the peak of my cheekbone. No doubt I'll scar and remember Nader every day of my life when I look in the mirror.

On a lighter note, it's the exact shape of Ohio. Like— identical. My eyeball is floating lazily on Lake Erie. It's thinking of going water-skiing later.

For dinner we eat food that tastes like we are visiting an old folks' home. The green beans are mushy. The chicken is covered in powdered soup mix and tastes like one big chemical. The milk is skim and blue. I suddenly miss my father. He may not say much or stick around when we need him, but the man can cook.

"We can't wait to take you two to the Grand Canyon!" Jodi says at dinner.

"You're gonna love it, Lucky," Dave adds. "It's a life-changing place."

Great. No pressure, guys.

The conversation—or should I say monologue—moves from tourist sites to Dave's crazy work schedule to Jodi and her seven new diets, which aren't working. She talks about how she can't exercise because of the ailments—a bad back, sore knees, breathing difficulties—all caused by her weight gain. She says she read in one of her magazines that people like her die young. She read in another that people like her go on disability and get to use the handicapped parking spots. She read in *Us* about the master cleanse diet, where you don't eat anything but just drink lemonade for two weeks. "Like that's even possible," she says.

Mom offers, "One of the girls I swim with in the winter does that master cleanse thing every year."

Jodi looks at her. "So?"

"Uh. I don't know. I mean, it works for her, but you know, not everyone can do it. I mean, uh." I've never seen Mom this awkward. "I couldn't, that's for sure."

Things go silent for about a zillion minutes. No one talks about my Ohio scab or my mother's amazing butterfly stroke. No one talks about food.

Jodi eventually says, "Lucky, I see you put clothing on the floor under the window. I put the little table next to the dresser for that."

"Thanks. But I'm cool with it being under the window."

"But that will mess up the energy," she says, a golf ball–sized lump of mushy green beans in her cheek.

I decide, even though I know all about feng shui from a book Mom has, to play stupid. "What energy?"

"The chi," she says while chewing.

"The what?" I ask.

"Chi!" she says, her mouth so full she has to tilt her head back to say it. Mom and I squirm. In the Linderman house, talking with your mouth full equates to peeing on the food.

To avoid having to see Aunt Jodi's half-chewed dinner again, we don't say anything else. I try to get another bite into my mouth, but each bite I chew hurts.

I wipe my mouth and thank them for dinner. "I hope you don't mind, but I need to go to bed," I say.

Mom offers a sympathetic smile. "Your cheek hurt, Luck?"

I realize my whole face is crunched up in pain, and I look more miserable than usual. "Yeah. It's killing me, actually."

Jodi gets up and comes back with two over-the-counter pain pills and takes my plate.

Dave drops his dish at the sink and says, "I've got to go back to the office for something. Back later." Then he rests a hand on my shoulder as he moves toward the door. "Tomorrow I'm getting you on that bench, man. In two weeks, you'll be beefed up and ready to kick that kid's ass."

Jodi answers, "Don't encourage him."

LUCKY LINDERMAN IS NOT
GOING TO STAIN YOUR CARPET

The first thing I hear the next morning is Aunt Jodi diagnosing me in the next room.

"But he's got all the signs, Lori!"

"You just met him yesterday."

"Still...he's depressed."

"He's jet-lagged and a teenager. He's fine."

"He's always frowning!"

"That's his *thing*. You'll understand when you get to know him better."

I hear one of them sigh. Then Jodi says, "Did you ever think that your marital problems could be rubbing off on him? On top of being bullied, that could really mess a kid up."

"There are no marital problems," Mom insists. "We just needed a break."

"Seems to me you're just ignoring all the problems in your life. Dave does that, too, you know. I just don't think it's healthy. For you or Vic *or* Lucky. I mean—"

"Please. Just stop. I have a lot on my mind right now," Mom says.

"He could be at risk!"

I can practically hear my mother's eyes roll. "He's not at risk."

"It's a proven fact that bullied kids are more depressed than non-bullied kids."

"He's not bullied."

"Didn't he get beat up? Isn't that what happened to his face? Isn't that why you're here?"

"Look. I mean this in the nicest way, Jodi, but could you please mind your own business?"

I hear Dave clear his throat.

"I am *not* turning a blind eye to a suicidal teenager," Jodi says. "What if he kills himself here? In our house?"

"Oh my *God*," Mom says. I hear her footsteps. The door opens. She sits on my bed. "Luck, get out of bed and act happy. Your aunt Jodi thinks you're going to kill yourself."

After Dave goes to work at eight, I pull out the book I brought with me, *Catch-22* by Joseph Heller, and sit in the living room. Mom goes swimming while Jodi sits in front of the TV watching talk shows and news flashes between thumbing her gossip magazines with movie-star cellulite articles. She sits forward for the entire Dr. Phil episode. Two college kids are explaining why they treat their girlfriends like shit, and when Dr. Phil gets stern with them, she cheers as if she's watching sports or something.

After her swim, Mom gets a bottle of pure aloe from Jodi and spreads it all over my cheek. I admit, it feels nice—cool and soothing—but when I look in the mirror, I see Ohio is coated in ectoplasm or frog spawn. I look like a freak.

The jet lag catches up with me during midafternoon, and I consider swimming to wake myself up, but when I go out, it's too hot to do anything but go back inside. How is this better than life at home? For either of us?

I decide to nap, even though it makes Jodi look at my mother and raise her eyebrows.

RESCUE MISSION #103— OPERATION RESCUE LUCKY

I am trapped in a grass hut with great energy. There is a mirror by the door, and two chairs facing east. This is feng shui prison. There are cameras. Dr. Phil is here. He's asking me how long Nader McMillan has bullied me.

"Since forever," I say.

"Can you be more specific?" he asks. The audience nods.

I sigh. "It started when he peed on me in a restaurant bathroom when I was seven." The audience gasps. "Then it just never stopped. Never."

Dr. Phil leans forward. "Who did you tell about this, son? Did you tell your parents? The teachers?"

I nod.

"I know it's hard to talk about, Lucky, but I need you to talk. Who'd you tell about the first thing? The urinating part?"

I shook my head. "I didn't tell anyone. My parents were with me. What could I say? I mean — I didn't pee on myself, right? Who would do that?"

"So no one stood up for you?"

I'm silent. I look up. The audience is taking notes on pads made from jungle leaves. The ants are wearing tiny white doctor coats and glasses low on their noses.

"How does that make you feel?"

"I don't know."

"Can I tell you how *I'd* feel if it were me?" Dr. Phil asks.

I nod because I feel hot tears forming behind my eyes.

"I'd feel really tired. And I'd feel that someone should be sticking up for me," he says. Then he stops for a second and he puts his hand to his chin and looks at the camera. "Do you know what I wanna know?"

I can't tell if he's talking to me or the audience. The jungle insects *zeep-zeep-zeep,* and a strange rodent scurries from one corner of the feng shui hut to another.

"I wanna know: Where are this bully's parents? Why don't they know he's been terrorizing Lucky for eight long years?"

The audience hangs on his every word. He looks to a different camera suspended from a boom to the left of the hut. "The sick thing? They *do* know." The Dr. Phil music cues faintly in the background. "When we come back, we'll have some strong words with Mr. and Mrs. McMillan, and we'll talk to Lucky's parents, too, so we can all make sure Lucky leaves our studio today feeling like someone cares."

The music gets louder, and Dr. Phil turns to me off camera. "Son, you need to find a way to get this out of there," he says, gently poking me in the heart. "You can't keep it all inside." All I can hear is what he just said to the audience. *Strong words with Mr. and Mrs. McMillan. We'll talk to Lucky's parents, too.*

I send a convoy of red fire ants on an emergency maneuver up the leg of Dr. Phil's suit pants. I give them orders to bite the minute he starts talking again, so I can get the hell out of here.

Then Granddad Harry swings in on a jungle vine and plucks me from my Dr. Phil feng shui stool and delivers us both back to the limb of our peaceful tree, side by side, swinging our legs, except Granddad is missing his right leg from the knee down.

"I love it here," I say.

He eyes me up, concerned. "You do?"

I refer to my dream physique with my hands. I am completely buff, wearing a sleeveless T-shirt, and my deltoids are firm, small cantaloupes.

"Oh, that," he says. "You'd give up real life and freedom for *that?*" He looks at me as if he's annoyed.

"What use is my real life? It sucks."

"Huh," he grunts. I realize that maybe that might be one of the stupidest things I've ever said. I mean, yeah, my life sucks. But his life sucks way worse. So I change the subject.

"I've been reading about you," I say.

"Am I in a book?"

"I've been reading the files Granny Janice kept," I say. I add sheepishly, "And your letters."

He nods and says, "You read those letters?" I suddenly feel awful about it. "Some nights I dream of her back when we met in high school. We used to go with our friends to this little diner every Friday night, and we'd show off our cars and eat hamburgers and French fries and try to score a bottle of beer." He laughs. "Just a bunch of know-nothing kids, before we realized what might happen to us."

"You mean the war? Getting drafted?"

He nods. "Janice wrote and told me we lost Smitty and Caruso in the first three months. They'd enlisted, you know? Caruso got blown to pieces by a mine, and Smitty got hit with friendly fire. Then me. The only person still standing from our original Friday-night crew was Thompson, who'd escaped the whole nightmare by having a bad back and flat feet."

"I have flat feet," I say because he looks so sad talking about his dead friends.

"Boy! We had some fun! Used to go out hunting and camping on weekends, and we'd smoke cigars and steal liquor from our fathers' cabinets." He stops and looks at me. "You do that kind of stuff, don't ya, Lucky?"

"I tried smoking once because Danny wanted to. I hated it."

"No hunting?"

"Nope."

"Camping?"

"Nope."

"Chasing girls?"

"Nope."

He looks concerned. "You got friends?"

"Kinda. Not really. I used to have Danny."

"What happened to him?" he asked.

"Nader turned him against me."

"That Nader kid is really screwing himself out of a good afterlife," he says. "Have you told any adults about this kid?"

"They're all afraid of his dad."

"What is he? Some sort of nut or something?"

"A lawyer."

"Huh." He sighs. "What about your dad? Can't he talk to this lawyer guy?"

I don't have the heart to answer this.

OPERATION DON'T SMILE
EVER—FRESHMAN YEAR

A month after Evelyn Schwartz went crying to the guidance department about how "morbid" my survey was, the Lindermans were called into a second meeting. All of my teachers were there, including Mr. Potter, my social studies teacher.

"He's got no problems in my class," Mr. Gunther, my algebra II teacher said. "I was going to ask him if he wanted to tutor after school for extra money." Mom and Dad raised their eyebrows and nodded. Of course, I'd say no to the tutoring because I didn't want to be in school late, when the Naders of the world roamed the halls in packs (also known as wrestling practice).

"He's doing fine in my class, too," said Mrs. Wadner—the best biology teacher in the world. If I managed a B, I'd be happy, because she was hard-core.

Each one weighed in with the same conclusion. I was doing well in school. I nearly smiled, but stayed loyal to Operation Don't Smile Ever and just nodded.

But then the Shrew got her turn. The Shrew was my gym teacher that semester, and she never smiled, either. She was short, had thighs the size of Pacific totem poles and a face to match. She wore the same outfit every day, only in different colors—a classic coach tracksuit with stripes, and a T-shirt that had something to do with Freddy High girls' sports.

"Lucky has been absent quite a bit from my classes this month. If he keeps it up, he'll get an F."

True, I'd hidden in the empty auditorium during a few gym classes since the locker-room banana incident.

Dad looked at me and said, "Well?"

"I just don't want to go into the locker room. You know. The rumors?"

They all just stared at me. No one nodded a knowing nod or made a face that showed they knew what I was talking about.

The final teacher was Potter. He said that since my first idea for my social studies project had been "not the most appropriate," I should come up with another.

I went into my backpack and pulled out the chart. "I'm going to do my project on the Vietnam War draft lottery and figure out how many people in my class would be drafted if it was 1970."

They all nodded. I looked at Fish. He looked to be about sixty. I said, "Were you born in 1951?"

His eyebrows went up. "Close. Fifty-five."

"What's your birthday?"

"February twenty-seventh," he said.

I looked at the chart and said, "Your number is sixty-six."

I turned to Mr. Gunther, who offered without my having to ask. "August thirty-first."

"Lucky you," I said. "Your number is two hundred seventy-five. Safe."

Mr. Potter looked impressed. Mom and Dad actually looked proud. This was just supposed to be a simple mix of skills for freshman social studies. Complete survey, make graphs, write paper, make speech. I could have easily counted the number of kids wearing blue one day, or the ratio of kids who ate French fries versus side salads at lunch. But I wanted mine to have an extra effect. I wanted to make people think.

Not to say my first question *didn't* make people think. It had. Totally.

I knew this because completed questionnaires from my first social studies project had started to show up in my locker. Like — a bunch of them.

Some were obvious jokes (two said they would masturbate themselves to death, one said he would opt for death by rabid livestock) and some weren't. Some mentioned shooting themselves with a father's gun or cutting to escape all the pain. Though our lockers at Freddy High weren't personalized in any way from the outside, people somehow knew to stuff these papers into mine through the ventilation slots. I thought about tossing them, thinking this was Nader getting his friends to mock me, but instead I saved them in the back of my social studies folder.

Then one day while I was roaming back to my classroom from a lav break, I saw someone standing next to my locker with a folded piece of paper in her hand. It was Charlotte Dent, a popular junior. (Popular in the infamous sense, not the cheerleader sense. If there was a bad rumor going around, there was a good chance it involved Charlotte.) The only true thing I knew about her was that she liked to push the boundaries of the Freddy High dress code by occasionally wearing too-short skirts, too-high heels and tank tops that were too tight. That day, she was wearing a pair of jeans and a Hooters softball T-shirt. I watched her insert the paper into my locker and walk away. I felt kind of honored that she even knew about me or my locker. Of course, I retrieved the questionnaire before I headed back to class.

The question read: *If you were going to commit suicide, what method would you choose?* Written in curlicue handwriting in pink ink, the answer read: *I'd shoot myself, but I'd shoot Nader McMillan first.*

LUCKY LINDERMAN CAN BENCH-PRESS
FORTY-FIVE POUNDS

I emerge from the guest bedroom with *Catch-22* under my arm just as Uncle Dave gets home from work. "Leave the book and come with me," he says.

Uncle Dave has turned his side of the garage into a weight room. He has a big hanging canvas sheet that divides the garage in half because Aunt Jodi insists that her side of the garage is reserved for her car, which is what garages are *for*, and scoffs whenever she refers to Dave's fitness regime.

Dave shows me around his free weights. "You get that recently?" he asks, looking at Ohio.

"Yesterday."

"Yesterday?"

I nod.

"Seriously?"

I nod again. I can't tell whether he knows that this is what my parents are fighting about or whether he's just figuring out that it might have something to do with it.

"Anyone particular do it, or just some random asshole?" he says, taking his place on the bench with a dumbbell in his right hand and curling it.

"Big asshole. Been bugging me for years."

"Did you hit him back?"

"Nah."

"Why not?"

"He ambushed me."

"Bummer. Next time you should hit him back."

"You think?"

He nods, counting his last ten curls internally.

"I dunno. My dad always taught me that walking away is better," I say.

"Has it made the kid stop picking on you?"

I shake my head. "Nope."

"Then I can't see how it's helping," he says. "Can you?"

"Not really."

I do a few curls and it feels good. Then he shows me how to do fly lifts for my triceps and deltoids. His dumbbells are way too heavy for fly lifts, so he retrieves a pink plastic pair.

"Jodi's," he explains. "Not like she'll ever use them."

He doesn't seem to see how emasculating it is for me to use hot-pink dumbbells, but I get over it. I figure maybe after a few days of these, I can work my way up to his manly ones.

After twelve reps twice, Dave invites me to lie on the

bench, so I center myself and get ready. Free weights kind of scare me, since I've only ever lifted weights on the machine in the weight room in the Freddy High gym. He pulls a few weights off his bar so I can handle it. By the time he's done, it resembles a little kid's barbell, with only two smaller weights on each side. I think it's forty-five pounds.

We're halfway through eight reps of benches when he asks, "Do you frown all the time or what?"

"I guess," I say.

"Why?"

"Why not?"

"It's a downer, for one thing. And how are you gonna attract girls by moping around all the time?"

I laugh on an exhale. "Heh. Girls. Yeah, right."

"What? They don't have girls in Pennsylvania?"

"Not really."

"So, what? You don't want a girlfriend?"

"Nah."

"Why not?"

"It's complicated," I say.

"You watch. When you go back and they see that scar on your face? You'll have to beat them off."

This is so funny I have to lock my arms and tell him to take the bar. "I can guarantee you the girls where I live will not want a piece of the boy who has Ohio permanently etched into his cheek."

"Ohio?"

"Yeah," I point. "Check it out. It's the exact shape of Ohio."

He stares at it and marvels. "Wow. No kidding."

Two minutes later he's helping me bench forty-five pounds three more times to "feel the burn," when Aunt Jodi comes to the door. It squeaks as it opens.

"Dinner in five."

"'Kay."

"Don't come in all sweaty."

"'Kay."

The first time I see Aunt Jodi the next morning, she's by the sink, downing a line of pills. I make a feeble wave in her direction and flop onto the couch with my book to wait for Mom to come in from her early-morning laps.

"Vitamins," Jodi says after washing the last one back and swallowing. "And for my back."

I nod and open my book.

"Be thankful that you're young. When you're old like me, everything starts going downhill."

I know that Aunt Jodi isn't even as old as Mom or Dad, but I just keep reading and hope she'll stop talking to me.

"Not just my body, either. My nerves are terrible. I never thought that would happen. Not after so many years of taking so much crap," she says. "You know, you're not the only kid who's been bullied. Try being fat and pimply your whole life."

I can't tell if she can see my face go red, but it does, and it makes my scab itch. I continue to pretend to read my book, which is impossible to do with the ants there, mocking Aunt

Jodi. They say: *Try being fat and pimply your whole life? How about she tries using that treadmill for once?*

She disappears for a while, and Mom comes in from her swim. After a shower she joins me on the couch. Jodi shows up soon after and flops onto the love seat.

"How's your book?" she asks.

"Good so far. Weird."

"Why weird?" Mom asks.

"Well, I'm only on the first chapter, but so far all I can understand is that there's a bunch of soldiers in the hospital because they don't want to fight, and then a guy from Texas comes in, and he's so nice he makes all the other characters want to go back to fighting the war."

"Huh. Sounds funny."

"I guess so." I move a pillow behind my head and close my book.

"Sounds morbid," Jodi says.

"Depends on how you look at it," I say. "I call it history."

"I guess it is history," she says. "And your family has had its share of that."

"That's the truth," Mom says.

"It's a shame," Jodi says.

"Why?" I ask.

Jodi sticks out her lower lip as though she's thinking really hard. "It's a shame because of what it's done to your family, for starters."

Mom picks up a random magazine from the coffee table and opens it to any page that isn't about our family.

"I like reading about it. It helps me understand everything a little better," I say. What I don't say: *It makes me feel like someone in our family actually gives a shit about what happened to Granddad.*

"As long as it's not making you depressed," Jodi says.

"He's not depressed," Mom says. She rolls her eyes at me.

The phone rings and Jodi looks at the caller ID and says, "It's Vic."

Mom says, "Tell him I'm not here," and goes into the guest room and closes the door.

Jodi lets the phone ring instead. "I don't lie to people," she says, giving me a look.

Mom and I switch between napping and reading (and swimming, for her) all day until Dave comes home. We go to the garage.

"Today is legs and back," he says. "You sore from yesterday?"

"Yep."

"Is it bad? I tried to keep it mellow."

"Nah. Not bad. Just a little stiff."

"How about Ohio?"

I almost smile. Almost. I manage a smirk and say, "Itches like hell."

We lift for forty minutes, taking turns on the mat with ankle weights and doing squats with the bar. Jodi pokes her head through the door as we're stretching out at the end.

"Dinner in five."

" 'Kay."

"Don't come in all sweaty."

"'Kay."

After dinner (frozen chicken Kiev, microwaved baked potatoes and cold carrot sticks) Dave and I slouch on the couch and watch baseball. I can talk whenever I want, not just during commercials, or not at all.

Aunt Jodi and Mom sit at the kitchen table, only feet behind us, and talk about stuff. Jodi mentions again that I could be "at risk" and that she knows a good local psychologist who might talk to me on short notice, and the ants jump up and down on the couch back screaming: *He can hear you! He's sitting right here!*

THE SIXTH THING YOU NEED
TO KNOW—THE NINJA

Aunt Jodi is vacuuming the living room for what seems like forever. Even after I emerge from the guest room and sit at the table, she vacuums. She keeps ramming it into the couch legs, which means she's probably looking at me instead of what she's supposed to be doing.

Aunt Jodi has arranged the breakfast cereal boxes from large to small on the table. The ants are lined in front of them, in the same big-to-small order, arms crossed, looking tough. I look at them and they wave. *Good morning, Lucky Linderman. How did you sleep? Still using those pink plastic weights?*

I wonder if the ants will ever go away. I remember wondering if my dreams would ever go away, too. Of course, they didn't. Maybe the ants are the second step toward complete Linderman insanity.

I pick out the Cheerios and pour them into the bowl at the only place setting left on the table. I fetch milk from the fridge, and on my way back I see Jodi just standing there watching me, with the vacuum on, but at a standstill, sucking the carpet right off the carpet.

When I sit down, I notice the pill.

The minute I notice it, I ignore it.

The minute I ignore it, Jodi turns off the high-pitched whir of the vacuum.

"How'd you sleep?" Jodi asks.

I nod to acknowledge her question. "I expected more traffic," I say, and cram some Cheerios into my mouth. Each bite makes my scab itch more. I chew in a way that makes me look crazy—moving my scabbed cheek in grandiose motions to scratch without scratching.

"Yep. It's quiet," she says. "Safe, too. Dave and I sometimes take night walks and we never see any funny business."

Funny business. It's like she wants to be old or something.

"You should try it," she says.

I nod. "I'll take one tonight—maybe Mom will come with me."

"I mean *that,*" she says, pointing to the pill.

"I don't take pills."

"Maybe it would help," she says.

I get up, take my cereal bowl to the sink and rinse it. "Maybe it wouldn't."

As I move to put my bowl in the dishwasher, she stops me. "I'll do that."

She opens the top rack, and I see that her dishes are also arranged in some sort of dishwasher feng shui.

Swimming is the only way to cope with being outside during the day here, even though chlorine is only going to dry out my scab. Staying inside for Jodi's morning TV routine is out of the question.

The pool is short, and I can only get in about five strokes of freestyle before I have to turn. Towels are unnecessary because the sun bakes you dry in about fifteen seconds...and then you have to jump into the pool again so you don't fry on the spot. How do people live like this?

The pill is still at my plate during lunch, but this time Mom sees it first.

"That's Jodi's seat, Luck," she says, and motions for me to move over.

"No. He's right," Jodi says as she walks from the kitchen, balancing an array of oven-warmed, odd-smelling food. She puts the greasy chicken nuggets in front of me proudly and adds, "What do you dip with?"

I don't eat chicken nuggets, but I know I can't be rude. "I'll take honey, please."

My mother is staring at the pill.

"Honey? Ugh! All that sugar is bad for you!"

I nod because I do not have the energy to educate Aunt Jodi on how if she's feeding me chicken freaking nuggets, most likely made out of the disgusting sphincter parts of hormone-injected, badly treated factory chickens, then a few tablespoons of honey are the least of our worries.

"What's that?" Mom finally asks.

I say, "A pill."

She gives me the look. The look says: *I know it's a pill, Lucky. I wasn't asking you.*

Jodi throws of couple of sheets of fake-looking "roast beef" on a piece of bread with some kind of white cheese product on top and warms it in the microwave. She tops it with ready-made gravy straight from a jar. Just watching turns my guts.

"Jodi?" Mom says, and Aunt Jodi looks up. "What's that?" She's pointing at the pill.

"That?"

Mom leans over, picks up the pill and holds it up between her index finger and thumb. "This."

"Just something to make him feel better."

"I feel fine," I say.

Mom is staring at Jodi, and Jodi is staring hard at the open-faced sandwich as she saws through it, puts half on a plate for Mom and sits down. She picks up her half, slops it through the blob of congealing gravy and shoves it into her mouth and takes a bite. While she's chewing, she finally looks up and acknowledges Mom.

"He's fifteen," Mom says, stone-faced. "Keep your pills away from him."

"I was only trying to help." While Jodi's talking, a bit of food escapes her mouth and lands on my plate, next to the lukewarm, nasty chicken nuggets that I am not eating. "It's just Prozac."

"He doesn't need Prozac."

Jodi puts her hand out toward Mom. "Give it here." And when Mom does, Jodi pops it into her mouth and swallows it.

Mom leaves her lunch on the table and goes back to her laps.

A few minutes after she's gone, Jodi says, "Does she always swim this much?"

"Yeah. It's her thing."

"Huh. You'd think she'd get sick of it."

"Not yet," I say.

"Weird," she says, gobbling the last of her sandwich and washing it down with a Diet Coke.

"Not for our family," I say. This makes Jodi laugh, and when she gets up to clear the rest of the table, she musses my hair a little with her free hand.

At midafternoon I take a break from my book and go to the guest room to use the bathroom, and I find Mom on her bed, gorging on a bag of granola, and I'm starving, so I eat some, too.

Between crunchy mouthfuls, Mom says, "I don't think you need pills. I mean—I'm worried about you, but not that much."

"I know."

"It wasn't her place to do that to you," she says. "She just doesn't think."

"Don't worry. I wouldn't have taken it."

"Good. But I want you to know I didn't tell her to do that."

"Well, yeah."

"I mean—I'm worried about you, but not that worried."

"You just said that," I say. The ants say: *Hey! Don't be a smart-ass.*

"I want you to get it. Do you get it?" she asks.

"Yeah."

"Good."

Then she looks at me, her eyebrows raised. "You're sure? I shouldn't be *worried* worried, right?"

"Right. Nothing to worry about. I'm fine."

Now. I'm fine *now.*

When Dave gets home, I lift weights with him. We do different muscle groups again so I don't hurt myself. When I sweat, it stings Ohio, but I don't care.

"You're digging this, aren't you?" Dave asks.

"I am."

"Only three days and you're already feeling great, am I right?"

"Yep."

It feels really good to release the built-up bad energy from the last eight years of my life. And it feels really good to spend time with a cool guy. He's not scared of what I might say. He's not afraid to give me advice. Already I feel something good coming from this. I find myself wondering what it would be like if I could trade Dad for Dave.

The ants say: *Be careful what you wish for.*

About ten minutes before we're done lifting, Dave goes

over to the tool bench by the door and clicks off the radio. Then the door squeaks open, and Aunt Jodi pokes her head in.

"Five minutes."

" 'Kay."

"Don't come in all sweaty."

" 'Kay."

As we shut down the garage for the night, Dave calls me over to the corner to show me a scorpion hiding behind a bag of pebbles. It's really small.

"Is it a baby?" I ask.

"Nope. That's full grown."

"Something that small can kill me?"

"Well, it can hurt you really bad, but it probably won't kill you. We have black widow spiders and rattlesnakes here, too, though. *They* could kill you."

"Huh."

I think of those microscopic things that killed so many soldiers in Southeast Asia. The parasites and bacteria and malaria. I decide if I was going to go, I'd want to be eaten by a tiger or something. At least I would know it was coming.

Ten minutes later, as I stare at a plate of so-called lasagna that once had freezer burn so bad that the top layer of noodles is still brittle and covered in a white film, I decide to share my I-just-saw-my-first-scorpion story, and though Dave told me it couldn't kill me, I say, "Seriously. I'd rather be eaten by a tiger than killed by something so small."

"See?" Aunt Jodi says to Mom. "You need to take him to see someone."

"I'm sitting right here," I say. "I can hear you."

"Good. Maybe you'll stop scaring your mother with talk of suicide."

I laugh. I laugh because what else is there to do? I can't keep up with Aunt Jodi's freaky mood swings. I don't know when I'm allowed to joke or be sarcastic. Okay, well, no. I know today I am not allowed. To joke. About being eaten by a tiger.

Too late.

Jodi looks horrified that I'm laughing.

"Lucky, stop laughing," Mom says, monotone.

I stop laughing and go back to frowning. I reach up and press on my scab where it itches the most. The urge to pick it is like nothing I've ever experienced. Mom tells me that I will probably have a scar anyway but that if I pick, half of my face will look blotchy, and I decide I'm weird enough already without being blotchy.

"I thought it was a funny joke, Luck," Uncle Dave says.

Jodi shoots him a look.

"What? A kid can't joke? One minute you tell him to be happy, and the minute he does, you say it's a sign that he's nuts? Sheesh. Make up your mind," he says. The ants form a rotating halo above his head. They sing that high-pitched note that angels sing.

I take my first Arizona night walk after dinner. The temperature is bearable. I couldn't convince Mom to come with me, but I'm glad. She was happy enough reading her book, and I need time alone after that dinner conversation from hell.

Everything street-side in this development is well lit. The only shadows exist close to homes, under cars and around the occasional tree or cactus display. I walk until I feel I've gone around too many corners, then turn back so I won't get lost, and then explore a different direction. I do this until I have walked three cul-de-sacs, and decide that I am too boring to live. The ants say: *You really are a mama's boy, Linderman.* I check my watch, and it's only been fifteen minutes.

I decide to be more exciting, and I walk without caring if I get lost. After another fifteen minutes, I am back on the road behind Jodi and Dave's house.

That's where I see the ninja.

She's nearly invisible, all in black, moving through the pebbled back-lawn areas parallel to me, from one little shadow to another, stopping occasionally to look behind her to check if she's being followed. When she turns her head, hair — so long and straight that it touches the asphalt when she's crouched down — flares out like a skirt would if she were spinning.

I slow my pace so I can see her next move. She darts from behind a parked SUV to the corner of the next house and then disappears behind it.

I slow more. I stop. I wait for her to appear again on the other side of the house, but she is gone.

RESCUE MISSION #104 — JUNGLE NINJAS

I am in the dark jungle, hiding behind a tree. I have a dozen burning-hot, greasy chicken nuggets in my pockets. I can feel the grease burning my thighs. Granddad is sitting under a small lean-to inside the camp perimeter. The gate is open.

After I've been there a few minutes, Granddad whispers, "You can come out now, Lucky. Frankie is sleeping."

I sit on the muddy ground with him and offer him the nuggets. I don't tell him that they are probably made out of chicken's assholes. I watch him eat them slowly — not at all like you'd think a starving man would eat. I put one in my mouth and chew it about a hundred times before my throat opens enough to swallow it.

In the jungle outside this little camp, there is movement. There always is. Birds moving at night. Snakes. Rats. Predators. Prey.

"Don't worry about them," he says. "They're probably running food or water or ammo. Probably digging tunnels right here under us. They're like ninjas."

Doesn't he know the war is over?

I hand him another chicken nugget and he eats it. "I hope you're eating better than this at home, Luck."

I want to tell him about how Nader beat me up again. I want to tell him about how Aunt Jodi thinks I should take Prozac. I want to tell him about the ants because I know he'd understand. He's got Frankie. I've got Nader. Maybe he even sees ants, too.

Right then I hear the leaves around me shuffle, and I see the vague outline of a person crouched down and darting through shadows of the jungle, her long, straight hair swaying behind her as she runs.

I swing my M16 into forward position and tell Grand-dad to get up and follow me. I eye Frankie, the sleeping guard. Personally, I want to shoot Frankie so he can't come looking for us, but I know Granddad has some weird bond with the guy, so this time I'm just going to sneak by while he's sleeping.

I do a quick limb check on Granddad, and he has every single one, so he's able to walk behind me as we navigate the path to our freedom.

We walk for an hour until I hear talking up ahead. We duck into the brush and listen. After a few minutes of silence, we continue on. Right into an ambush.

Two ninja-like soldiers in pajamas like Granddad's come at us from behind. One takes Granddad down. Before the other one can floor me, I turn the M16 around and plunge the bayonet right into his skinny little torso.

His friend has his arm around Granddad's throat. I real-ize neither man was armed with anything but themselves. He's saying something to me in some Asian language. I can't tell what it is. I don't care. I stab the bayonet into the nearest enemy body part—his leg—until he lets go of Granddad, and I tell him he can run away if he wants.

As I pull the rifle up to my shoulder to shoot him in the back, Granddad says, "Don't."

I say, "Why not? He was gonna kill you."

"But he didn't."

I look at him and shake my head. "I don't get it. How am I supposed to rescue you if you won't let me?"

• • •

Mom is snoring, which I don't think I've ever heard before. It's kinda cute. And then I realize that there are cold, greasy chicken nuggets in my bed. I'm holding one, too. I must have squeezed it during my fight with the ninjas because it's complete mush now. I collect the nuggets and take them to the bathroom and flush.

THE SEVENTH THING YOU NEED
TO KNOW—JODI GETS WEIRDER
ON WEEKENDS

Dave and I hang out all day in the garage. Apparently, this is what normal men do on Saturdays. He washes his car in the driveway and moves a few things around in the garage for a while and then washes Jodi's car. He has a few boxes he's filling with junk he doesn't want anymore—books, beer steins and cassette tapes he says are from college. I'm doing a few fly lifts with his dumbbells now. I had to take the weight down, but at least I'm not using the hot-pink ones anymore.

"Can I ask you something?" he says.

"Sure."

"Remember when you told me that you don't think about girls?"

"I didn't say that," I say. "I said they're not into me. I think about girls all the time."

"You're right. Sorry. So—don't you think they'd notice you more if you smiled and seemed happier?"

"Girls are a pain," I say. "All they do is rag on each other and gossip."

He laughs. "Not all of them."

I don't feel like getting into it, so I keep lifting and counting.

He sits down on the bench and stares across the garage for a minute or so and then says, "Your mom is worried about you, Lucky. She wants me to find out if you're okay. I mean, she doesn't think you're ready to jump off a cliff or anything, but she's your mom, you know? She has a lot on her plate right now."

"Yeah."

"So?"

"So what?"

"Are you okay?"

I look up and keep my mouth straight. "I'm as okay as I can be, considering I live with my parents."

"Yeah. I remember not liking my parents at your age, too."

"I like them, but I wish they did their job, you know?"

He shakes his head and chews on his lower lip and looks at me, which tells me he doesn't get it at all.

"My dad won't talk about anything. I mean, he'll talk about food, but at home if we try to talk about anything real, he just gets up and walks away."

"I never saw your dad walk out on any conversation any time I knew him."

"Yeah. In front of other people, he's perfect. But really, he storms out more now than he ever did."

Uncle Dave sighs. "Huh. Why do you think that is?"

"I dunno. Probably because he's still messed up by what happened to his dad. I mean, that's obvious, right?" I point to my POW/MIA shirt.

"I don't know, Luck. I get that he's messed up, but I'm thinking this is more about the shit that's going on at school. With this kid. When you're a parent, you have to deal with more serious shit as your kids get older. I think he's not sure what to do. He didn't have a dad to show him how it's done, you know?"

"Yeah, but I can't see why that's my problem and not his. I mean, it was their choice to have a kid. He should step up."

Dave nods and shifts his lips around. "So what about your mom?" he asks.

"She basically does what Dad tells her to. He's not really all that nice to her, either. I mean, when it comes to me. I think they were probably fine before I was born," I say.

"Do you want me to talk to her?" he finally says.

"No. We have an understanding."

"So…"

"So what?"

"Do you want me to talk to your dad about it?"

"I don't want you to talk to anyone about it. You asked me why I don't smile and I told you." Of course, this is not the real reason. The ants say: *You're a liar, Lucky Linderman. Tell him about the locker room. About what Nader does to snitches.*

"But I want to help."

"You are helping."

"Really?"

"You're helping me a lot more than anyone has so far."

I point to the bench. Even though I know I should wait until tomorrow to press again, I really just want to do a few reps. My chest is sore, but it makes me feel like I'm doing something. *Something.* Which is more than I've ever done before.

On Sunday we are startled awake by Aunt Jodi zipping open the curtains and saying, "Time for church!"

Mom says, "Not for us, it's not," and turns toward the wall.

Jodi says, "Sorry, kiddo, anyone staying in this house goes to church on Sundays. Period."

I wonder which pill has made her like this. After just a few days, I know the blue ones make her weepy, and the white, diamond-shaped ones make her mellow. I wonder which one makes her a church freak, because up until now I wouldn't have pegged her as someone who was so hard-core about Sunday mornings.

Mom is sitting up now, glaring. "Don't call me kiddo."

"Fine. Lori. Sis. Whatever-yer-name-is. We leave in an hour for church," Jodi says in the scariest chirpy voice I've ever heard, and before she walks out the door, she straightens the hanging mirror and pretends to shine it a little with her forearm sleeve.

Mom is boiling. This distracts me from the fact that I'm boiling, too, because when Jodi barged in, I turned my head too quickly and left the corner part of my aloe-coated Ohio scab on my pillowcase. I get up and inspect it in the mirror. It's now the exact shape of West Virginia. (Which means the scab left on my pillow case is a slice from Toledo to Cincinnati, straight through Dayton.)

"You okay?" I ask as I press a tissue to the bleeding ex-Ohio.

"Yeah, I guess," Mom says. "You go ahead and take a shower. I'm swimming first because *my* God lives in the pool."

After my shower I realize that unless I plan on wearing a pair of camouflage combat shorts, then I'm screwed for church pants. Jodi told me that everything in Arizona is casual, but somehow I doubt she meant going to church dressed like a walking army-navy store.

I figure Dave might have something around that would fit me, so I put on a plain T-shirt, wrap my bottom half in a fluffy white towel and go in search of decent pants.

I find Jodi in the kitchen. "Do you think Uncle Dave has any old dress pants that might be close to my size?"

She is stunned. I figure she's happy I'm showered and getting ready to go to church. I figure she's proud that I've come to ask for more respectable clothing. Problem is, I've just caught her downing a handful of pills. A big handful. More than ten. I'm guessing they were pills she shouldn't be taking, because she's staring at me still, ten seconds later, trying to figure out what to do.

"*Dave!*" she yells—like, *yells*. And then she shields her eyes from me, as if I'm standing here naked. She overreacts so much that I peek down to make sure Mr. Lucky isn't poking out or anything, but of course he's not. I'm wrapped in two layers of towel.

Uncle Dave shows up, and she says, "I think Lucky was just about to show me his...his...penis!" She breathes dramatically, simulating hyperventilation, with her hand (the one that just tossed all those little pills into her throat) on her chest.

I look at Dave and shrug. "I don't have any nice pants. I figured you might have something that fits me."

While we're digging through his closet, he asks, "You weren't really going to flash my wife, were you?"

"Uh, no way," I say. "Why would I do that?"

"Yeah. I know," he says as he finds a pair of slacks that are too long but small enough to nearly fit my waist. "She's got a heckuvan imagination." The ants say: *Imagination? The woman is bat-shit crazy.*

I'm not sure now is the time to say this, because I've only been here five days, but I say it anyway. "I worry about the pills."

He nods, still eyeing up the pants. "Yeah."

"Belt?" I ask.

He finds a belt and gives it to me.

Mom walks into the guest room just as I'm looping the belt. "That was nice of you to make the effort, Lucky. More than I can do."

We drive to church in Jodi's SUV, and the vibes are weird. Dave isn't saying anything, as if he's being forced into this like we are. A few times Mom and Dave meet eyes while Jodi talks about the Grand Canyon. It's as if they have sibling ESP, because I can tell they're communicating without saying a word. I've noticed that when they're in the same room, they don't talk much, but they exchange these looks. Being an only child, I have no idea what they're saying or what it's like, but it looks cool.

The church is a big, open warehouse with pews. It's like no church I've ever been to before. It feels like Wal-Mart or something. Not to say it's not pretty. It is. The windows are huge and stained glass, and the walls have tapestries and paintings and sconce lights. The pews are uncomfortable. We manage to squeeze into one about midway up the aisle, and while Jodi talks to people around her, Mom, Dave and I sit and leaf through the little programs we picked up at the door. Jodi doesn't introduce us or even acknowledge to these church friends that we're her guests. She's high-energy, like maybe those pills I caught her eating this morning were speed or something.

Eventually the music starts, and the pastor gets up and starts to talk, and Mom and I slouch in the pew and endure it. The local news about deaths and illnesses of members of the congregation is interesting. The youth chat—about abstinence and how rap music promotes swearing—is okay. But the scripture goes on forever. I start to daydream. One minute I'm staring at the stained glass, and the next minute I'm in the jungle.

RESCUE MISSION #105—BAITING THE TRAP

I am with Jodi, Dave and Mom. Mom has on a full ninja suit—all black and tight-fitting. She has a mask on, too, so only her eyes show. Jodi is fatter here—the jungle mocks her.

She can't walk without tripping, because she can't see her feet. She is being eaten alive by mosquitoes and other flying and biting insects. She has on her typical Arizona outfit—shorts and a tank top. Not jungle-friendly.

She curses and slaps at mosquitoes on her arms. "Damn! I should have brought that Avon stuff!"

Mom darts behind a tree and reaches into her ninja suit, produces the Avon stuff and hands it to Jodi, who slops it onto her arms.

Dave is in front with me. We are scouting. With each step I look down to avoid booby traps, and then I look up, waiting for Granddad to appear on a tree branch or swing in on a vine.

But so far there is no evidence of a camp or Granddad anywhere.

Jodi yells, "Wait up!" and we all shush her.

Dave continues to walk ahead, crouched down. Then he stops and points. I catch up and look. We've found it. The main camp. We drop to the ground.

"What's the plan?" Dave asks.

I have no plan. I've been rescuing Granddad for eight years, and still I have no real idea of a plan.

"I say we use Jodi as bait," I suggest.

"I was just thinking that," Dave answers.

We tell her to walk around to the front. We tell her to act like a lost American tourist. She sees no problem with this and comments, "Maybe they'll have a soda machine in there. I'd kill for a Diet Coke."

Mom is nowhere to be seen. She has perfected ninja.

Dave and I watch as Jodi waddles around to the front of the camp, and just as she's about to get to the gate, she is eaten by a hole in the ground and begins screaming a wild, high-pitched sound that is pure animal. Dave flinches. I hold his arm, a command to stay still, and we watch as all of the camp guards arrive outside the gate to see what they've caught in their trap.

The novelty of a fat, middle-class American woman is too much for them. As she screams, they point and laugh. One of them reaches in and steals her backpack and starts rifling through it.

Dave and I sneak in the back entrance.

"Lucky!" Granddad says. "You brought a friend!"

"Let's get out of here, Granddad," I say. "Come on!"

He points to his feet, which are gone from the ankles down. He says, "Did you know that in Vietnam, the number of soldiers who suffered complete crippling or amputation of the lower limbs was three hundred percent higher than in World War Two?"

• • •

I wake up to singing and clapping. There is a mosquito on my forearm, and I quickly cover it and squash it.

The youth choir is up onstage now, in flowing white gowns, and they're singing something in the key of goose-bumps. To look normal, and less like a kid who was just in the jungle twelve thousand miles away, I stand up, like everyone else, and I start to sway and clap, too, even though I feel like a complete spaz and I have to look at other people to see when to clap. The ants say: *Dude. You have to copy off people to* clap? *What's* wrong *with you, kid?*

That's when I see the hair. The long, straight, perfect, swaying hair. The girl from the shadows — my real-life ninja. She sings in the church choir.

When the service is over, Aunt Jodi schmoozes. She's unbearably upbeat and alert. Feisty, even. She makes it her business to tell each singer that the performance was wonderful. She tells parents that their children were "so well behaved!" even if they fidgeted through the whole service. Dave, Mom and I stay sitting in the pew, and Mom and Dave say a few small-talky things to each other.

Then Jodi approaches the parents of my ninja girl.

The family forms a small defensive circle, and Jodi touches the shoulder of the husband and says, "Virginia just keeps getting better! You must be so proud!" While she says this, she reaches out for Uncle Dave's hand and yanks him to standing.

Ninja Mom says, "Oh, hello, Jodi. How nice to see you."

Ninja Girl has these huge green eyes. So green I can see them from here. And her hair is even more amazing this close up. She's like a girl from a commercial.

She notices me looking at her and I try to make a half smile so she doesn't think I'm a perv. She looks back at me. I can't read the look on her face. She seems amused by something, but she's not smiling at me. The ants say: *She's so out of your league that she's playing a completely different sport.*

Jodi continues to squeeze Dave's hand, even though he's awkwardly squished between her and the back of the closest pew and staring to his left, at the pulpit. "Wasn't she just amazing, Dave?"

"Sure," he says. "She's just amazing." I think I'm nodding at this.

The ninja family starts to walk down the center aisle, and Jodi follows them. She lets go of Dave's hand and continues to talk to them, even though they're using every.single form of negative body language to make her go away.

I don't even pretend not to watch Ninja Girl walk by me and up the aisle. She glides by in her choir gown — easily five foot ten, which makes me a dwarf, but who cares? I don't think I've ever seen anyone so mysteriously awesome in my whole life.

I'm not sure what Jodi says that makes them all look back at me and Mom, but when they do I lock eyes with Ninja Girl again, and she gives me a strange look. I can't describe it. It's pity or something. She looks at my pants and how they're rolled up at the bottom. She notes my sneakers. Then she looks at my scab and makes a face like she's amused again.

"Come here, you two. I want you to meet these folks!" Jodi says.

I have no idea what pill makes her use the word *folks*, but I want to make sure I never take one of those.

Mom is pissed now. She has the same look on her face that she had during the stupid school "expert" meetings. The same look she gets when Dad says all those things he says. *Don't keep asking him if he's okay. You'll only make him feel worse about it.*

"Hi," I say. The family is polite, and they ask me if I'm enjoying my vacation. "Yes," I say. Then Ninja Dad says, "We have to get Virginia to her next appointment. Excuse us," and they walk over to the pastor at the front door and start talking to him. Rather than wait in line behind them, Jodi turns and tells us to follow her out the side door, where we came in. I look back at Ninja Girl, and she's still looking at me.

When Mom asks Jodi why she didn't go out the front door, Jodi answers, "Closer to the car." But I saw she didn't put any offering in the plate. And I saw she didn't sing the hymns. She's using the side door because she doesn't want to see the pastor.

She's not here for God. She's here for some other reason.

For Sunday dinner, I decide if I'm going to be stuck here for two more weeks, then I'm going to eat better, even if I have to cook it myself. I teach Jodi and Dave how to make and grill basic homemade hamburgers out of some ground beef she'd been saving for a from-a-packet casserole. I show Jodi how to chop an onion correctly. I explain the acceptable ratio of meat to bread crumbs. It's as if all those years watching the Food Channel actually taught me something. I mean, something other than the fact that the Food Channel is not a magical tool to bond sons and fathers.

Dave perfects the toasting of buns on the top rack of the grill. I show him how to burn off the extra crud before he turns off the flames, and just as he's about to put the finished burgers on the plate the raw ones were on, I save the day and get a new plate and explain the basics of raw meat and cooked meat, and how the two should never be in the same place at the same time.

During dinner Jodi says, "In my family, boys weren't allowed near the kitchen."

Mom grunts, "Shame."

"You know, it *is* a shame." She looks at Dave and says, "No offense."

"I wish I'd have learned this stuff, too," Dave says. "I'm happy to be the provider, but if anything ever happened to Jodi, I'd be living on frozen meals."

Jodi laughs. "Dave—you already *are* living on frozen meals."

Wow. Self-awareness. I wonder what pill she took for that.

He laughs. "I guess I am."

Jodi chews a bit of her burger and says, "You know, maybe God sent us Lori and Lucky because he knew we had to learn to take care of ourselves better."

Oh. I get it now. God had Nader beat my ass and my mom leave my dad just so Jodi could learn how to chop onions and use a propane grill. Great. Awesome. The ants hold a protest on Dave and Jodi's side of the table, complete with picket signs that read: AUNT AND UNCLE FAIL. THESE PEOPLE SUCK. I'M WITH STUPID.

While Jodi and Mom clean up, Dave and I lift and listen to the radio. Every burning muscle in my body wants to ask him about the ninja girl, but I don't. And just when I work up the guts to say something, he says, "I have a big meeting tomorrow, and I think I need to hit the office tonight, just to make sure everything's set." Then, still sweaty, he jumps into his car and drives off.

I can't figure him out. One minute he's the only sane man in my family; the next minute he's gone, just like Dad.

It's long past dark, and I don't see anyone walking tonight. Maybe Sundays are off-limits. Maybe my ninja girl even goes to bed early and gives her swaying, beautiful hair a break. I wonder where she sneaks off to. I wonder, does she have a secret boyfriend or a favorite place? The ants say: *What the hell are you doing to yourself? You'll never see her again. She lives two thousand miles away!*

Then I think of Granddad and wonder why I dream about a man who is twelve thousand miles away. It makes me ask: Why do I care so much about people who are so far away from me?

OPERATION DON'T SMILE
EVER — FRESHMAN YEAR

My draft lottery graphs worked out great. Thirty-six percent of responders had birthdays that yielded eligible draft numbers in the 1970 lottery. This helped me prove my point, which was: A lot of people got drafted only a few decades ago. I planned to say this in my speech. "Look around the room. Imagine over a third of us gone."

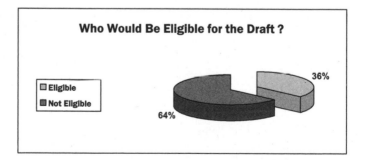

Who Would Be Eligible for the Draft ?

☐ Eligible
■ Not Eligible

36%

64%

The two extra-credit graphs I made proved that my generation doesn't understand the draft lottery at all. Only 16 percent of responders answered yes, claiming they knew what the draft lottery was. Sadly, 70 percent of that 16 percent didn't actually know. Most thought the draft lottery "had something to do with winning money."

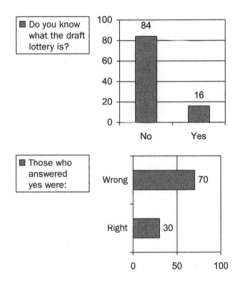

The only thing left to do was make my presentation. Most of the kids in my class had already presented their original projects. Every Friday since the new semester, we'd listened to people telling us results of their random surveys and I learned interesting facts about my classmates. I learned that 87 percent of them didn't wash their hands after going to the bathroom. Fifty-four percent didn't wear seat belts when they didn't have to. Seventy-six percent felt they should lose some weight.

Sixty-seven percent didn't like math. Fifty-two percent hadn't read *Romeo and Juliet*, our freshman English assignment. (Of them, 78 percent watched the movie.) Only 24 percent had ever gone camping. And only 21 percent felt they had a good relationship with their parents.

Count me among the 79 percent who felt they didn't.

I tried to keep Dad updated on my social studies stuff because he seemed so into the idea when we had the meeting with my teachers. Since then he'd tossed out a bunch of suggestions and stats, like, "Don't forget to tell 'em that the total number of drafted in Vietnam was about 1.8 million" or "Make sure you tell 'em that sixty percent of soldiers killed were under twenty-one."

His numbers were accurate for the most part, but the more I researched, the more I learned that Dad's belief that the whole country disrespected Vietnam vets was largely in his head. Left over, I guess, from what Granny Janice had seen all that time she fought for the lives of MIA soldiers. Or maybe left over from what he felt himself.

"How's the draft lottery thing coming along?" he said during the second week of February.

"Good," I said. "Speech on Friday."

"Did you do the graphs on the computer?" Dad asked.

"Yep."

"I'd love to see them," he said. But of course he wasn't around before Friday for me to show him the graphs before my speech.

On Friday, I did my presentation quickly, flashing my

three graphs up on the screen and concluding that kids should really know about the history of the draft, and what it would mean for them, because *they* are the ones who'd be drafted if it ever happened here again. At the very end, I mentioned a little bit about our modern-day selective service program and put up a link to the website in case anyone wanted to research that themselves. There was barely a clap in the room when I finished.

After my next class I went to my locker and found another suicide questionnaire inside. It said: *If you were going to commit suicide, what method would you choose?* The answer read—in all block capitals and black Sharpie marker: *I'D DRAFT MYSELF AND GET MYSELF BLOWN UP BY A TERRORIST BOMB. MAYBE THEN MY FATHER WOULD NOTICE ME.*

I admit, I thought it was a clever answer.

When I was finally able to show the graphs to Dad that weekend, he didn't have much to say except, "Nice graphs, Luck." I pointed out that I'd used the 1970 lottery as my example and showed him the table with the numbers and the birth dates. All he did was nod. I guess it was hard for him to look at the logic behind the draft lotteries, because that same logic had taken away his father. And, anyway, what's so logical about the day you were born deciding when you might die? That's just a cruel joke, as I see it.

16

LUCKY LINDERMAN IS IN AISLE SEVEN

I want to make dinner tonight," I say at breakfast while Mom crunches some granola cereal and Aunt Jodi fiddles with her hair and browses through a *People* magazine. It's not even eight yet. My body is still on Eastern time or something.

"For who?" she asks.

"For us," I say.

"All of us? A whole dinner?" Jodi asks, amazed, as if I've just turned into a llama or a giant hot-air balloon. As if I didn't just teach them how to make hamburgers yesterday.

"Yeah. Something homemade."

Mom grunts in assent while reading about trans fat on the back of her cereal box, and Jodi works herself into a huff.

"I've never been so insulted!" she says, and storms from the dining area and out toward the pool.

Mom walks out to the patio, where Jodi is sitting. I didn't mean to insult her. It's not like I told her to her face that she can't cook. But she can't, so I can't see the big deal.

At about nine, the doorbell rings, and I open the front door to see the UPS man holding a package a little larger than a toaster. He asks me to sign for it.

"No problem," I say. He's staring at my scab. I wonder if he can see West Virginia. I sign and hand the little machine back and smile at him, and the scab cracks a little and I can feel it seeping either blood or that oozy scab stuff as the pizza-oven air hits my face.

"Who was that?" Jodi asks as she and Mom come in from their long talk on the patio.

"UPS."

"For me?"

"For us. From Dad."

Jodi inhales as if she's about to say something moody, but instead she says, "How sweet!"

I open the box and hand a wrapped present to Mom, who winces a bit because she knows Dad well enough to know that whatever is inside the package will embarrass her, be of no interest to her or be the wrong size. This isn't a put-down. It's a family joke. Well, if you can find it funny. But I think since she refused to "take it anymore," this is not a funny joke at all. It's just another reason to be in Arizona while he's in Pennsylvania.

Dad included a POW/MIA T-shirt for Jodi and one for Dave. Jodi holds it as if I just gave her a dead man. Away from her body. Like it smells. In a way, I guess I did just give her the body of a dead man. *Welcome to the life of a Linderman, Aunt Jodi, where every day is a funeral we never had.* The ants say: *And shh! Make sure you don't talk about it!*

"I'm sorry I got so mad before. It's that time of the month," she starts, and I can hear Mom groan quietly from across the room because she'd never say that. "I'd love for you to make dinner tonight. Your mom has volunteered to take you to the store for ingredients."

I say, "Great. Makes me feel like I can pay you back for letting us stay here."

This sentence somehow brings us all back to reality. My mother and I look at each other like refugees and then look at Aunt Jodi. She pities us and we can feel it.

Mom unwraps her present. It's a box of melted chocolates. After a morning in the back of a UPS truck during the Arizona summer, I'd call them liquid chocolates. She goes to throw them away, but Jodi insists on putting the box in the fridge, claiming, "It'll still taste like chocolate even if it isn't pretty!"

The ants climb into the shipping box full of packing paper and search around. One returns. *Linderman, the gift accounting command has confirmed negative gifts for you. Sorry, son. Your father sucks.*

The grocery store is freezing cold. Mom is shivering. The ants are shivering. One of them is handing out tiny scarves to the others.

I decide to make yogurt-and-red-pepper-marinated chicken, cherry tomatoes and pineapple shish kebabs. Mom seems impressed. This is the first moment I realize that I have never actually cooked a whole meal by myself. Sure, I mixed a lot of banana muffin batter when I was seven, but this will be a bit more than pouring a bunch of premeasured ingredients into a bowl and stirring. Still, I'm confident. I've watched enough *FMC* to know how to make marinade, cut chicken and cook rice. It's not rocket science.

The first thing Aunt Jodi says when she sees our groceries is, "Rice? We don't eat rice!" I think of what Granddad Harry would say about rice after thirty-eight years of eating rice.

An hour later she eyes the bowl of chicken marinating in the fridge.

"Wow. What *is* that?"

"Marinade."

"Why's it look like yogurt?"

"It *is* yogurt."

"Huh," she says, and shakes her head. "Yogurt on chicken. This will be an interesting night."

At dinner Aunt Jodi is eating so fast she doesn't stop to speak. Dad says a quiet meal is the best indication that you cooked well. I think this is probably the quietest meal my aunt Jodi has ever participated in. I allow Dave to take partial credit because he turned the meat when I told him to, and brushed on more marinade. He even changed plates from raw meat to cooked meat, so he's learning.

After dinner we meet in the garage, and he spots me as I

do ten reps of fifty-five twice, the most I've ever done. I tell him that he's the coolest guy I ever met.

"Thanks, Luck," he says. "And you're the coolest kid I ever met."

"Yeah, right," I say, chuckling.

He puts the bar up and says, "What? You think you aren't cool because some asshole tells you you're not?"

I want to tell him that he really doesn't know me. That I'm not very social. That mostly I read books and keep to myself. Instead, I point to my cheek. "Did you notice it's West Virginia now?"

He squints and cocks his head slightly to the right. "My God. Look at that."

"Weird, isn't it?"

We go back to lifting. I'm doing squats with his big dumbbells, and he's benching. I say, "So you really think I should hit him back?"

He finishes his press. "Depends."

"On what?"

"You ever hit anyone before?"

"We have one of those big punching bags in the gym at school. I hit that once."

"Is he big?" he asks.

"Yeah. He's a wrestler, too. He'd probably kill me."

"Or pin you to the ground in an act of homoerotic bliss."

I say, "Yeah, right."

"Can I tell you a secret?" he asks.

I nod.

"When I was in school, I was a bullying asshole just like that kid."

Not what I expected. I expected the opposite—a heart-to-heart between victims.

"But the only reason I treated other kids like shit was because I was jealous of them." He shakes his head. "I didn't have the guts to be independent or smart. I was too scared to do anything different, so I beat up on the kids who had guts. Sounds pretty pathetic, doesn't it?"

"Yeah."

"Remember that when you see that guy again. He's gutless. He only picks on you because he's jealous." I nod at this, but I can't figure out what Nader McMillan would be jealous about. The ants say: *Certainly not your ability to cook basmati rice. Frankly, it was starchy and too sticky.*

I make him spot me for ten more reps, and I can feel the scab crack a bit with my exertion, but I don't care. Today made me feel awesome. I cooked a kick-ass dinner and lifted fifty-five pounds thirty times. I celebrate by going night swimming.

I dive to the bottom of the deep end and I smile—a real smile, not a fake-for-Jodi-smile—for the first time in six months. When I do this, it makes me laugh underwater, and an eruption of bubbles races me to the surface.

I dry off and lie on a lounge chair at the side of the pool. I stay completely still so the motion-sensor light goes off.

The stars glow brighter and it's beautiful. I hear kids a few houses away talking. I hear TV intro music. I hear an occasional car drive around the block, and the background hum of the highway that leads to town. I focus on the common area behind the block of homes, where all the scrubby backyards meet, and I see a group of shadows moving with lit cigarettes. I squint and I see teenagers holding hands and kissing and doing the stuff normal teenagers do.

When they're gone and I'm about to get up, I see her again — the shadow with the long, swaying hair. She's scurrying through the landscape like a trained soldier.

I sit up without thinking, and the bright spotlight goes on, reflects off the pool and blinds me.

RESCUE MISSION #106—TIGER INTERROGATION

I'm strapped to a chair, and two blinding lights are in my face.

"Where is she, Lindo-man?"

Something punches me. My mouth is full of hair. I can barely breathe.

"You tell us where she is, and we let you see your grandfather," the voice says.

I squint and see it is Frankie, the guard from Granddad's prison camp, but then he's a tiger. A beautiful orange-and-black-striped tiger. His coat is so shiny and perfect I want to reach out and pet him. His jowls are huge and house teeth so big I can't look away. This is, without a doubt, the most stunning creature I have ever seen.

"You like the taste of that, Lindo-man? There's more where that came from."

He holds up another clawful of hair. It's long, straight and perfect. It sways.

I spit the hair out of my mouth and look around the room. We're alone — just the tiger and me.

"I don't know where she is," I say.

The tiger laughs. "Why you protecting her? She enemy! She eat you! She worse than us!"

"She's not the enemy, dipshit. You're the fucking enemy," I say. Behind my back I am trying to undo the loose knot in the leather strapping they have used to tie me to the chair. I have my thumb in the knot now. Shouldn't be much longer.

"Dipshit?" The tiger backhands me and nearly knocks me and the chair over. In the process he gives me a scratch across my forehead, and I'm pretty sure I dislocated my thumb from the force. I coax the thumb out from the knot and wiggle my wrists. Looser. Looser.

I lunge at the tiger before he knows I'm free, and I wrap the leather strap around his neck and pull and twist until he can't breathe anymore. I straddle him and pull for what seems like five whole minutes, and even while he dies and his eyes roll back and he pisses on the concrete floor and his huge pink tongue rolls out, he is still beautiful — and I feel bad for having to kill him.

When I'm sure he's dead, I get up and take a pistol from a table by the door and make sure it's loaded. I look in the drawer of the same table and find an extra clip, and I bring it with me. I have no idea what's outside the door, so I consider this a search and destroy from the minute I get into the hall.

It's empty. A long hallway lit by three tiny lightbulbs.

"Granddad!" I yell. I don't give a shit if they hear me. I'll kill them all.

"Lucky!"

I run toward the voice. He says it again. "Lucky!" I'm closer.

The end of the hallway is dark. I've got my pistol aimed at the final door.

"Lucky!"

I kick it open and scour the room with my weapon, and there is no one except Granddad, tied the same way I was, with a leather strap, to a chair. He is missing his left forearm, so they tied him at his armpits.

"Oh, thank God you're alive," he says as I untie him.

I ponder this. *Thank God I'm alive? Really?*

"I killed the tiger," I say. "I'm sorry."

He says, "Sometimes we have to do ugly things."

I take him by the right hand and pull him out into the hall. "Stay close," I say. "I'm getting you out of here."

"Your head is bleeding." He leans down and rips off a strip of his pajamas. I stop and tie it around my head.

I run, crouched, to the opposite end of the hallway, where the exit door is. I open the door slowly and peek out. There is no one. No vehicles. No nothing. It looks a little like the abandoned warehouse down the road from the Freddy pool. I point in the direction of a flying American flag—the flag that flies over by the pavilion at the pool. "This is it!" I say. "We're home!"

I look behind me to see him — freed. But he is not there. I turn in circles. He's gone.

"Dammit!"

• • •

I say this out loud and wake up both of us — me and Mom. She groans and turns over. I go to do the same but instinctively reach up, where the black headband Granddad just gave me is still tied around my head.

"Dammit!" I whisper again. I nearly had him.

THE EIGHTH THING YOU NEED
TO KNOW—GINNY CLEMENS

We've agreed that today is for making Jodi's pool area a happier place. Right now it looks like the one room of the house where no one goes. Because it is. The paint is chipped, and the patio has gaps and cracks and crooked spots that need to be smoothed. Before he left for work, Dave helped me carry all the extra bags of pebbles out there so we can make the little cactus area pretty again.

The scrambled eggs I make for breakfast taste so nice that Jodi eats Mom's portion while Mom does short laps in the pool. "And all you put in here was salt and pepper?" Jodi asks.

"Yep." I fake-smile at her. I fake-smile pretty much every time I'm near Jodi, even though it hurts my now cracked and peeling cheek, because I can't tell what she'll do or say next.

"Who'd have thought it was so easy?" she says. "They're delicious."

An hour later Mom has scoured the scum line along the pool gutter and is fixing the small garden areas with a tattered exercise mat under her knees. Jodi is scrubbing down the dusty lounge chairs with a blue scrub brush, and I'm filling holes in the patio area with dyed cement.

As I near the side of the garage to mix a little more cement, I overhear Aunt Jodi talking to Mom about me. She says, "He's so, he's just so, uh, *strange*! I mean, what fifteen-year-old boy *cooks*? He's not *normal*. And he has that look on his face! It's like he's forcing a smile or something," she says, as if this is the number one problem—what my face looks like. "I really think he's going to hurt himself, Lori. And you never know—all these school shootings...he might decide not to go alone."

Only two hours earlier she was telling me how great I was because I could cook eggs. Now my egg-making means I'm a homicidal maniac. Now I might wipe out random people at a mall because I don't smile enough. Why are the adults in my life so determined to bring me down when I'm feeling good?

I find myself thinking that it would be nice to be able to fix my life the way I'm fixing the patio. I wonder, is there enough terracotta-colored cement to fill the hole where my father should be? Or where my mother's spine should be? Or where my guts should be?

I think back to the last time I told Dad about Nader and

what he said. "Son, there will always be bullies in your life. Some people just don't know how to act."

Always? I know this sounds totally stupid, but sometimes I really can't see the point in living if I will always have to deal with this crap. I know I will have better times in my life, and I might even make myself into someone important, but if the whole time I have to deal with assholes, then what's the point?

I know if I said this out loud, Aunt Jodi would call an ambulance or something, but instead of shutting me up over it, why can't they just *answer me*?

I think it's because they feel bad for not making it fair. Rather than actually fix it, they freak out on kids who say things like, "I'd rather suck truck fumes than go through one more day of this place."

Hasn't everyone said something like that at least once? And really — I *would* rather suck truck fumes than deal with this sort of shit forever. Mom says that Nader is a loser who will grow up to be a loser and that I'll understand when I'm forty. But I want to understand *now*.

For dinner we eat frozen enchiladas that aren't half bad. Mine has rogue jalapeños in it, but I deal. I chew, I sweat, I wash them back with water. I am in serious need of a walk when I'm done rinsing the dishes.

I wear my earphones and rock out tonight while I walk. It's nine thirty and it's still a harsh hundred degrees. As I round the last corner, I feel a tug on my arm. I'm startled out of my walking trance and turn off the music with my thumb.

It's her. My ninja.

"Are you doing anything?" she asks.

I don't know what to say, so I say, "Just walking."

"What happened to your face?"

"Nothing." Dumbass. It's pretty obvious that something happened to my face. I just don't know what else to say.

"You get beat up?"

"Yeah, kinda."

"I heard from my mom that you're staying with Jodi and Dave because your mom left your dad."

"Yeah, I guess that's part of it. Not all of it."

"She said you're from Kentucky or something."

"Pennsylvania."

"Oh." Silence. I'm staring at her as if she's just beamed down from space. My throat closes up a little bit because it knows if I talk, I will say something that will make her hate me or notice I am not in her league. Though I guess that's pretty obvious already. "How old are you?" she asks.

"Fifteen. Almost sixteen," I say, even though it's a lie. I'm nine months from sixteen. "You?"

"Seventeen."

"Cool," I say.

"So if it's not all about your mom leaving your dad, then why are you here?"

"Well..." I blush. I feel like a complete sissy. "I dunno. I got beat up by this kid who won't leave me alone, and my mom was sick of 'taking it,' whatever that means." I put air quotes around *taking it*.

I realize that we're now walking toward a darkened gap between two houses. "You're not an asshole or anything, are you?" she asks.

"Uh — no?"

"You don't sound sure."

"I guess I'm not," I say, completely blown away by how crazy this is. How beautiful she is.

"Come with me," she says, and runs between two houses and across the road. I follow her. She is dressed all in black with a light, long-sleeve hoodie on top, and as she runs, the hood falls to her neck and her hair escapes. She cuts between two more houses, past a barking set of dogs, and then jumps a three-foot-high wall like a gazelle. Her hair jumps with her, a wave of silk.

We reach a playground, and she sits on a swing. She has to move her hair or else she will sit on it. I reach the swings and sit on the one next to her and catch my breath. By this time she has a cigarette in her mouth and is lighting it with a match. We're sitting there, her smoking, me watching her smoke, and it's too quiet, so I do what I've done my whole life when it's too quiet. I say something really stupid.

"You shouldn't smoke."

She sneers at me. "You shouldn't lie about not being an asshole."

"I didn't mean it that way. I just. I meant that — uh — you don't seem like a smoker to me."

"It's how I rebel," she says. "You'd do it, too, if you were me."

"Huh," I grunt. I cannot, for the life of me, figure out what the world's most awesome and beautiful ninja girl would have to rebel against.

"So why'd you come all the way out here? Why not some relatives in Kentucky or something?"

I can feel myself trusting her too much. I try to keep my mouth shut because the ants are telling me: *Stay safe, Lucky Linderman. Keep your mouth shut.* But I talk anyway. "My mother is a squid, so we had to come here because Dave and Jodi have a pool, and my mother has to swim several hours a day or else, as a squid, she will die. My father had to stay in Pennsylvania because he is a turtle and can't face anything other than boneless chicken breasts and organic vegetables."

My ninja is smiling at me. "Your mom is a squid?"

"Psychologically, yes."

"And your dad is a turtle."

"Right."

"What does that make you?" she asks.

"I don't know yet."

She takes a long drag on her cigarette. "You're interesting," she says.

"Thanks," I say, because I don't know what else to say. Because I'm too busy staring at her perky, little upturned nose and the silhouette of her lips as they wrap themselves around the filter end of her cigarette.

"Will they miss you if I take you with me?" she asks.

"What?"

"Can you come out tonight with me?"

"When will I be home?" The ants bury their faces in their hands. A beautiful seventeen-year-old girl wants to take me somewhere, and this is the best I can come up with?

"Before midnight, Cinderella."

"Where are we going?" The ants say: *Wasn't your first question dumb enough, Linderman? Sheesh. You're a real buzz kill.*

"Rehearsal."

"Oh," I say.

She answers, "How do you feel about vaginas?"

I stare at her and rehear that question about seven times. *How do you feel about vaginas?* I hear a car coming down the road toward the playground and distract myself from the question because I have no idea how to answer it.

"Well?" she asks.

"Well—I like them, of course," I say.

"Them? You mean vaginas?"

"Yeah."

"So if you like them, why can't you say it?"

"I just did."

"I mean the *word*. Vagina. You know?"

I am now sweating. It's so bad I feel sweat dripping down the back of my arm. I think the one and only time I ever said the word *vagina* was in health class in eighth grade. As in: *What is the name of the birth canal?*

She's right in my face, blowing smoke while she talks. "Vagina! Vagina! My God, what is so wrong with that word? It's just a body part! Can you say *tonsils*? Can you say *elbow*?"

I see the car parking in the playground lot, and I feel like something bad is going to happen. I don't know what to say to Ninja Girl. Frankly, I'm a little scared of her. She's ranting now. Pacing.

"Every five minutes on TV, I have to hear about erections that last more than four hours, and yet nobody can say the word *vagina*! It's crazy!"

I see the car doors open, one by one. I imagine four Naders. "Shit," I say.

"Shit? Why 'shit'?"

"Maybe we should get out of here," I warn.

"Why?"

"Those guys are getting out of their car, man."

She laughs. It comes from her throat. It's deep and sexy. "Those *guys*" — she places finger quotes around the word — "are my friends."

"Oh." I relax. "Good."

"So are you going to say it?"

"What?"

"Vagina."

"Oh. Sure," I say. "Vagina."

She grins and claps her palms together quickly, as if she's just won a round on a game show or something. This is the exact moment I realize we haven't traded names.

"What's your name again?" I ask.

"Ginny. You?"

"Lucky."

"Seriously?"

I nod. She laughs, grabs me by the POW/MIA T-shirt and says to her approaching friends, "Hey, look, guys! I just got Lucky!"

Four minutes later I am squished into a car with five girls. Three of them have crew cuts, so I thought they were guys at first, which I think I should keep to myself. Ginny is next to me, and I can feel the heat of her leg through my combat shorts. This is not the moment to think about her naked. And yet, I do.

So I am squished into a car with five girls — three of whom have crew cuts — and I now have a boner. The ants say: *Jesus, Lucky Linderman. Can't you control that thing?*

I start to think of everything I can to get rid of it. Nader. Aunt Jodi. My mother. My grandmother's funeral when I was seven. My granddad Harry. Jungle diseases. Amputations. None of it works, so I pray we have a few more minutes of driving before I have to stand up again.

"Do ya?"

I'm snapped out of my ugly-people-places-and-things visualization by Ginny asking this over and over. "Do ya? Do ya? Do ya?"

"Do I what?"

They all laugh like I just told a joke. I feel like I got away with something.

"Shannon says you probably wanna do Ginny."

"Oh," I say, nodding. "Uh — well. Not really."

They all laugh again. Ginny looks at me, hurt.

"Well, I mean, I would if I thought about that kind of

stuff, you know? But I'm — uh — not uh ..." How do I tell a carful of girls that I'm a virgin?

"He's a virgin," Ginny says.

"I am not!" I say.

"Oh boy! You are the biggest virgin I ever met," the girl next to me says. She pats me on the knee. "It's okay. We're all virgins."

"Virgins who love to say vagina," Ginny says.

They chant it together. "Vagina! Vagina! Vagina!"

In my life I've been cursed with crazy dreams about booby traps and prison camps and frog rain and amputees and talking tigers, and yet nothing I ever dreamed can compare to this.

A half hour later I'm sitting on the ceramic-tiled floor of the local rec center, and in the next room my five new friends are rehearsing a play called *The Vagina Monologues*.

When they told me the name of it, I wasn't sure what to say. Luckily, I didn't have to say anything. "It's a play about how our vaginas are always controlled by men," Ginny explained. "But we're here to take back control."

One of the girls said, "Fuck yeah!"

"Just sit here. We should be done in an hour," Ginny said.

"But —"

"You can see the show next weekend with everyone else."

"So why'd you bring me along, then?"

"It's better than walking around the block ten times a night, isn't it?" she says. "Or spying on people from your aunt's patio."

At first I listened through the door, but between the traffic outside and the hum of the central air-conditioning, I missed every second word, so I gave up. All I know is that the play has something to do with vaginas — which, I have to admit, are beginning to interest me.

By eleven fifteen, I am pissed off that they brought me here only to sit around and do nothing, and I feel trapped because I have no idea where I am and no idea how to get home. I feel like the stupid little kid again — just the way Nader makes me feel — so I prop myself into the corner and see if I can find Granddad.

RESCUE MISSION #107 — LAO RIVERBOAT

I am in a PT boat drifting down the Nam Ou river. The water is muddy and reddish, and Granddad is sitting cross-legged in the bow. He is so skinny I can see every sinew under his skin. He is brown from the sun and white from malnutrition. He has open sores in various places. He is missing an arm this time.

I am compact, squeezed into a corner in the stern of the boat, using the walls like a blanket. I am dwarfed by the cliffs on either side of the river. The river is so calm; there is nothing but peace here. How did everything become so quiet?

I suddenly realize we are alone. There is no guard. I get up and pad over to Granddad Harry. I look down at myself and notice I am in better shape than any other dream so far. Even my hands are muscular.

"Did we escape?" I am torn about what I want him to say.

"In a way."

In a way?

"Are we going home now?" I ask.

"Not quite."

"Where are we going?"

"To pick up your friends."

"I don't have any friends." Do I? I think about Lara and Danny back in Freddy. They aren't really my friends.

"Then we're going to have a party. Dancing. Feasting. Laughing."

Of course, he's delirious. That's the problem with being trapped in the jungle for nearly forty years. A person can't do that shit without going crazy.

I suddenly hear distant yelling. It is my five new friends — nameless except Ginny and Shannon. They are standing on a jagged bit of rock at the river's edge, smiling at us.

"Over here!" Shannon says. She is waving her arms back and forth over her head.

"Help!" Ginny says, her hair swaying behind her.

Granddad uses a long stick to push the boat toward them. I don't see until we get closer that two of the girls are completely naked. I am not aroused by this.

As we secure the boat to the small wooden dock below the rocks, the boat becomes a ferry. It just grows. I look up and Granddad Harry's arm is back. He's wearing a Navy-type uniform, like he's the ship's captain. I see I'm also in sailor clothing, including shined shoes.

As we help them aboard, they change, too. Ginny's tattered black pajamas turn into a tight-fitting pink beaded ball gown. Shannon's makeshift rice-sack dress transforms into a fluffy, frilly dress I can't ever imagine her wearing. The crew-cut girls experience the same magic as they board.

Old-time music, the kind Granny Janice used to listen to, plays through the ferry's speakers, and I'm the first to sit down because I've never danced in my life.

"Come on, Lucky! Dancing is the cure!" Granddad says.

He has two girls—a crew cut and Shannon—and they move gracefully in circles, as if they've done this with one another a million times. It's beautiful. Shannon's dress is flowing behind her. Granddad is laughing so hard his face looks forty years younger.

"Come on!" he says.

I stand up and hold my hand out to Ginny and the other two crew cuts. We form a dancing circle, the same as the others. I don't step on any toes. I don't trip or stumble or fall. When the song is over, another big-band number comes on, and I continue to swirl and spin and move my feet. I feel free. I dip the girls. I spin them. I spin myself. I bow. I am a movie star.

While we're dancing, Ginny looks at me right in my eyes, and I realize she can see into my future. She can see who I will be, not just who I am.

Then there is an explosion.

Have you ever felt the concussion of a bomb landing nearby? It is like nothing else. It is the instant delivery of hell. It is like everyone you ever knew dying.

• • •

The rehearsal room door slams shut, right next to my head.

I'm awake, and the girls are walking past me toward the main exit. When I look up, I see the girls are talking to me, but I'm nearly deaf from the explosion. I shake my head and swallow. Through the crackling in my ears, I hear Ginny say, "We're hitting McDonald's before they drop us off. You hungry?"

"Yeah," I say. An hour later the girls drop Ginny and me off at the playground and make a date for a dress rehearsal on Friday.

They drive off, leaving the two of us alone in the dark playground. As Ginny walks across the soccer field, she lights a cigarette and tosses the spent match.

"What was the driver's name again?"

"Karen."

"Karen," I repeat, trying to separate her from the other two crew cuts, but I can't.

"The one with the nose ring is Maya. She's Puerto Rican," she says.

"I didn't even see her nose ring," I say.

"You sat across from her at McDonald's for, like, twenty minutes, and you didn't see her nose ring? Damn. You're not real observant, are you?"

At McDonald's, all I could do was picture all five girls in their ball gowns, on the ferry on the Nam Ou river.

"So Maya and Karen and Shannon and—uh..."

"Annie."

"And Annie."

"Yeah. Her name is a sick joke. She has red hair and she was adopted. Get it?"

I don't get it. This must be obvious.

"Little Orphan Annie?"

"Oh. Yeah. That *is* a sick joke," I say. "Is that why she shaves her head?"

"What?" This isn't an *I didn't hear you* kind of "what." This is a *what the fuck did you just say to me?* kind of "what." I am instantly aware I said something wrong. "What did you just say?"

"I meant—uh—does she shave her head because she doesn't want anyone to see her red hair because her name's Annie. But now that I said it—uh—out loud, I'm seeing how stupid that is."

"Why do you care so much about hair, anyway?"

"I don't."

"You don't?"

"No."

She takes a long drag and tosses the butt to the side of the road. "So you don't like my hair?"

"Your hair is awesome."

"Yeah, it is," she says. "It's the only part of me anyone cares about, though."

I don't answer at first, until I realize she's waiting for me to say something. I say, "Why do you think that?"

"Jodi didn't tell you about me?"

"No. Should she have?" I ask.

"Oh. Well, it's not a big deal or anything, but I model."

I nod. Of course she does. Look at her.

"But just my hair. My hair models. The rest of me rebels," she says. I want to tell her that her face and her legs and her perfect hands are also model-worthy, but I figure it's probably a bad thing to say.

We come to the place where we have to split up. I have to somehow get into Jodi and Dave's house undetected at two in the morning. Ginny has to turn into a backyard ninja. The last thing she says to me before she runs off is "I really want you to come to the show. Think you could swing it?"

"When is it again?"

"Next Friday and Saturday."

"Sure," I say, and then she is gone.

LUCKY LINDERMAN NEEDS
SERIOUS HELP

Before my shower the next morning, I stare at the scab in the mirror. It's still the exact shape of West Virginia, but it's healing and peeling at the edges, and with each application of aloe, I can feel parts of it getting ready to flake off. The worst and thickest part, right over my cheekbone, is the exact shape of the Monongahela National Forest, too. I swear — I am not making this up.

In the shower, I think back to last night. Did I really go out with five girls? Five older girls? I retrieve their names. Ginny, of course. Shannon. And I remember Annie now, because of the story Ginny told me. The other two will have to be called Crew Cut in my head until further notice. The ants, who are lined up on the shower rail, say: *Your memory sucks, Linderman.*

When I come out of the bathroom, I check my watch. It's eleven thirty. This has got to be the latest I've slept in months. My muscles are still stiff, but it feels good to be stiff. I get dressed and stop at the mirror to apply more aloe, and I slowly flake off the edges of scab that seem to want to come off. When I'm done, it's the shape of Michigan. The mitten-shaped part, anyway.

I decide I should move my clothing to where Jodi wanted it—to get the good energy flowing in the room. I feel pretty positive today. I feel like a kid who has a friend. A kid who has a life.

And then I walk into the living room to find three people I've never seen before sitting next to Mom and Aunt Jodi, whose eyebrows form a concerned frown, staring at me.

I try to convince myself that these people are just visiting friends. But I learn through Jodi's introductions that they are professionals Jodi has called in to help me. With that look on her face like someone peed on her granola, Mom makes the motion for me to sit down in the only chair left empty.

After a week of forced fake-smiling, I let my face fall into its natural scowl. I feel like going animal on these people—picking more of the scab and eating it, and then blowing my nose into my sleeve. I feel like squatting on the coffee table and taking a shit on the latest *People* magazine just to give them the show they came for. *Crazy Boy Saved by Local Woman. Future School Shooting Averted.*

"Do you always wear baggy clothes?" one asks.

"Do you always sleep this late?"

"Do you have trouble sleeping?"

"Do you eat three meals a day?"

"Are you bullied?"

"When was the last time you remember being happy?"

"Have you ever thought about suicide?"

"Didn't you get in trouble at school last year?"

"What activities do you enjoy?"

"Do you have a job? What chores do you do around your house?"

"Why are you wearing that shirt? Do you support the POW/MIA cause?"

I am a shitstorm of sniper fire. "I *am* the POW/MIA cause," I say.

"There's no need to be hostile," one of them says.

I think Mom is smiling a little bit. She's always known me as the gutless boy who said yes to everything. (Son of gutless woman who says yes to everything.)

Jodi piles the last question onto the heap. "And where were you last night?"

I almost tell them about Ginny, Shannon, Annie and the two crew cuts—about the word *vagina*—but I don't want to get the girls in trouble. So I lie.

"I walked to the playground and was looking at the stars, but I fell asleep. If you want, I can tell you what I dreamed about," I say.

Right when Jodi is about to answer, Mom says, "Lucky has a habit of falling asleep like that. He's just a daydreamer. It happens all the time back home."

"Have you ever taken him to a doctor for it?"

Mom holds her face in a relaxed smile, even though I know she's dying to burst out in peals of laughter. "For what?"

"For this sleep disorder."

"Disorder?" she says, and then swats it away with her hand and a smirk. "I don't think so. I think he's a perfectly normal teenager."

"I can check him out if you'd like," the only man present says. I assume he's a doctor. I hope so. I've never had a complete stranger offer to "check me out" before.

"No, really. He's fine," Mom says.

"He's not fine if he's staying out all hours of the night!" Jodi says. "I think Elsa's right. I think he has a disorder!"

I sit forward and say, "I may be weird, but at least I'm not a drug addict, like you are."

The adults are stunned. The ants give me a standing ovation.

"Is he always this rude?" Elsa asks Aunt Jodi.

Mom says, "Lucky's never been rude. Not even when he should be."

Jodi sucks her teeth.

"What?" Mom asks.

"I got all these people here to help him, and you don't even care!" Jodi throws her hands up in the air.

"Who asked you to? And who said he needs help? He's a good kid! And what do you know about kids, anyway?"

Jodi turns purple. Like, beet-purple. "How *dare* you!"

Mom rolls her eyes.

"If this is the kind of treatment I get for opening my home to you in your time of need, then —"

Mom interrupts and smiles at the three bystanders. "I had to *beg* my brother to get her to say yes." She turns to Jodi. "And you've treated us like nothing but a burden since we got here."

I am already in the guest room, packing. It's some sort of reflex. I know I can't go anywhere, but I'm packing anyway. The door is open, so the conversation trickles in . . . just without me.

"I suppose trying to do the right thing isn't enough for some people," Jodi says, and then she bursts into a quiet sob.

After a few seconds Mom says, "You shouldn't have sprung this on us without asking. Lucky's fine. And you'll be fine, too, once your friends leave and you can go and pop all those pills you need."

When Mom and I are in the guest room with the door closed, I hear Jodi defending her pill use to her friends. "It's not like I'm freebasing cocaine, you know. My doctor told me I need them for my nerves." She adds, "What my sister-in-law didn't tell you is that she's probably half the problem. Spends more time in my pool than with her own son." I smile at Mom, who is not smiling. She's sitting on the bed, wringing her hands.

"You shouldn't feel bad," I say.

"And yet I do."

"We can just go to a hotel."

"Dave won't let us stay at a hotel."

I sit next to her. "Dave isn't our boss."

"Hotels are expensive."

"Not as expensive as living with Frau Nutcase on Planet Moody."

She laughs a little.

"Seriously," I say. "I'm considering getting hooked on her pills just to survive two more weeks of this. I'll pay the hotel out of my lawn-mowing money if you want. I have two thousand dollars."

She sighs. "We can't. Dave's my brother. We'll just have to work it out once those weirdos leave."

"Creepy."

"Yeah," she agrees. Then she turns to me and says, "Lucky?"

"Yeah?"

"What did you mean when you said you *are* the POW/MIA cause?"

I think about it. "I dunno."

"No, really. You can tell me."

"Really. I don't know what I meant," I say. "I guess I meant—uh—I was born with a POW/MIA patch on my skin or something, you know?"

"Do you want me to get Dad to..."

"No," I answer before she can finish the thought. "I like it. I believe in it. I know in my gut that Granddad Harry is still there."

"You do?"

"Don't you?" I ask.

She thinks and nibbles on her lower lip. "I'm not as sure as you are," she says. "How can you be so sure, anyway?"

"I just am."

"I worry about you," she stutters. "Those nightmares you have. The things I find in your room." I can't believe she has finally said something about this. It's like she's been a silent accomplice to me all this time, without a word. Still, I can't tell her.

"No need to worry about me. I'm fine. Promise."

"Good," she says.

After a few seconds of silence, I say, "Can I ask you something?"

She nods.

"Why didn't Dad pick up Granddad's case when Granny Janice died? Doesn't he care what happened? Doesn't he want to find out?"

Mom sighs. "You don't know what it did to him, watching his mother beat her head against a wall for thirty years. He just burned out," she says.

"I don't get it. He burned out not doing anything?"

"Just watching was exhausting. Broke his heart," she says. "And when she died, she *still* didn't have any answers. He just couldn't bring that with him."

I make a halfhearted nod, as though I understand. I guess I do. But I still don't understand why, if he left all that behind, he's still so messed up.

The conversation in the living room is getting louder. I think I hear Jodi say, "I am not a drug addict!" and it breaks our serious mood. It's like Jodi threw her own intervention. Mom and I snicker a little.

"So, seriously—did you really fall asleep at the playground last night?"

"Uh—yeah." This means no. She knows this.

She looks into my eyes. "Just be careful, okay?" Then she strokes my cheek—the healing one—and she says, "Damn. You're bleeding a little," and hands me a tissue.

The ants say: *Aren't we all bleeding a little?*

THE NINTH THING YOU NEED TO KNOW— BRIGHT ANGEL TRAIL

We leave for the Grand Canyon at five in the morning. Dave drives while Aunt Jodi stays particularly quiet in the passenger seat, aside from yelling at other drivers.

"Jesus! Take it easy!"

"Why are you in such a hurry?"

"How about a turn signal? It's the thing that happens when you use that stick on your steering column!"

Mom and I are in the backseat, and though I brought my music and my book, I'm not plugged in to either. I'm just looking out the windows, taking in the terrain. For a while it looks a lot like driving through Pennsylvania. I expected deserts and cacti, but it's fir trees and tall grass, only the grass is browner.

My mind wanders to Ginny. Last night I leafed through a few of Jodi's magazines and found one of Ginny's shampoo ads. She does the Favors from Nature line. She looks even more amazing in the pictures, where the motto, IT'S ONLY NAT-URAL, floats in bold type above her beautiful head. If you look at that picture, it's hard to imagine she's hanging out with a bunch of crew-cut feminists who chant "vagina." But maybe that's just a weird thing for anyone to imagine, no matter who's in the picture. I wonder what they're doing today.

"I didn't expect so many trees," Mom says after we pass through Flagstaff and continue northwest. Only ten minutes after she says it, everything flattens, and we hit a desert-looking place with mountains in the distance. "Maybe I spoke too soon," she says.

Finally, after four hours in the car making occasional small talk, we pass a sign that reads GRAND CANYON NATIONAL PARK.

We have to drive another ten minutes to see the canyon for real. It really is the most mind-blowing thing I've ever seen. Mom even cries a little, it's so amazing. All we can say is "wow."

Mom says, "Wow."

I say, "Wow, wow, wow."

The first look is overwhelming — an audible gasp sort of overwhelming. I can't really process what I'm seeing. It's almost like being underwater — at one of those underwater paradises, like the Great Barrier Reef, that you see on TV documentaries. Everything's enormous and a blur, a beautiful blur, and I feel weightless, unattached, or floating or something. As if the Grand Canyon is making me drunk.

The ants say: *What did you expect? It's the Grand-freaking-Canyon!*

Dave stands on Mom's right, and Jodi stands on my left. They don't say anything, but when I look at Jodi, she smiles at me and nods back toward the view and pats me on the shoulder.

We turn back on the road we came in on and follow it to a small village where our hotel is. It's the oldest hotel around, and it has a view of the canyon, which seems to be rare or something, because Dave says it was hard to get a room here on short notice, but he has connections. He checks us in, and we make our way to our rooms.

Only outside the two doors is there an awkward moment when we suddenly don't know who's rooming with whom. Dave gravitates toward me and says, "I think we should room together, Lucky," but then Jodi pulls him back and makes him open their door, and Mom and I do the same.

I realize now that maybe this whole Arizona trip was so I could bond with a man. Maybe one of the school "experts" told Mom this was a good idea. Or maybe Mom thought it up herself, or maybe Dave doesn't really think I'm cool but is just saying it because he's been given a job. The job is to make Lucky Linderman normal. Or make sure he's not going to really kill himself. Or get him to smile. By the time I get into the bathroom for a pee and a glimpse at my scab, I'm paranoid as hell that they've brought me to the Grand Canyon for some weird manhood ritual.

An hour after lunch, Dave and I walk into the canyon on Bright Angel Trail. The path is steep but not too bad. The brochure says this hike should take four hours. I've decided to forget about my paranoia for the afternoon.

Until Dave starts talking while we're resting on a rock halfway down.

"Wanna tell me where you were the other night?" Dave asks.

"Huh?"

"When you disappeared."

I don't say anything.

"I know you didn't fall asleep in the park, man."

"I did," I say. "Seriously."

"Dude. Come on."

I sigh. How the hell am I going to explain the vagina thing to Uncle Dave?

"I met this girl and we went for a long walk," I say. "Don't tell them, though."

He slaps me on the back so hard I think I might go flying over the edge of the rock we're sitting on. "A girl!" he says.

"Not—uh—a girlfriend or anything. Just a *friend* girl. And her friends."

"And her *friends*?"

"Yeah."

He laughs and shakes his head. "Give a kid some weights, and next thing, the girls are crawling on him."

"It's not like that," I say.

"You just don't understand girls yet."

"No, seriously. It's nothing like that."

He nods and says, "It's not that I don't believe you. I just know women."

I stand up and decide I'd rather walk more than talk about this. I don't appreciate that he's turned my secret into a big bragging point. It wasn't one. I'm at the Grand Canyon. I want to see it, not sit here and talk about stupid stuff with yet another person over thirty who doesn't get it.

We get to the mile-and-a-half rest area in about two hours. There's a bunch of tourists packed inside a small open-sided shelter, enjoying the shade. After we get a drink, we turn around and start back toward the trail, and some guy says, "You going back already?" He then explains that if we keep walking, in just a few short minutes we'll get the best view we ever saw, so we take him up on it.

And the view really is worth it. The sky is a deep blue and the canyon is endless. Really endless. I feel swallowed, but it feels good. I feel I'm as small as I should be. Smallness feels right somehow. Because if Nader McMillan was here, he'd be small, too.

Dave says, "Did I piss you off?"

"Nah."

"I did, didn't I?"

"Just don't tell them where I was," I say.

"Trust me. I won't."

"Good."

"Can I ask you a dumb question?" he says.

I nod.

"I keep hearing you came out here to see us because you were thinking about killing yourself. That true?"

I don't like the way he worded that. *I* didn't come out to *see* anyone. If I had it my way, I'd be playing gin with Lara Jones right now.

We sit on a shady spot of dirt, and he passes me the canteen we're sharing. "I don't mean to pry. I just want to know what's going on, you know?" he adds.

"I wasn't thinking about killing myself. I was joking about it. I got caught, and they're acting like I'm fucking crazy now."

"Joking?"

I tell him the whole questionnaire story and how the school overreacted and how I got questionnaires all the way up to the end of school in my locker. I told him about how no one gave a shit about what was really going on at the school — just about stupid made-up shit like this.

"So school hasn't changed much since I was there, I guess."

"Still sucks."

"Yeah," he says. "Well, it's good to know you weren't really considering it. I mean, that's a pretty final answer to any problem."

"Yeah, right?"

"You know you can call me if you need to talk about that other thing, too, right?" he says. "Or if you want to ask anything about your secret girlfriends." He laughs and I do, too, just to make him feel okay about having to say all that crap.

As we make our final ascent, I suddenly love Arizona. I love that Mom thought it was a good idea to just pick up and leave. I love Dave, who is turning out to be the father I never had, and I even love Jodi, although she's kinda crazy. I don't miss the Freddy pool or Lara or my own bed. I do not miss my father, which is a sad side effect of his being a small, fleshy creature who hides in a shell, thinking about menus all the time.

LUCKY LINDERMAN IS STILL TRYING TO DESCRIBE THE GRAND CANYON

We check out of the hotel, and then we drive around the rim for picture taking. Mom and I take turns trying to find words to describe how completely awesome the Grand Canyon is. In the end we both fail, and we go back to watching the sky.

"I can't get over how it changes color," she says.

It's true. One minute the sky is orange and red. The next minute it's purple and blue, and the next minute it's just like regular Pennsylvania sky, but bigger. All depends how and when you look at it.

We get to a popular parking area, and there is a bunch of college kids with their college T-shirts on. We stay to the right of them, and Mom and Jodi take pictures of the views, but then the group of kids gets loud.

"Go ahead! Don't be a pussy!"

Two guys are standing at the edge, eyeing a skinny walkway of rock that leads to a small rock platform about three feet away from the edge. It's like one of those cartoon images — a stalagmite of rock that supports a platform where the Road Runner would stand to taunt Wile E. Coyote. The skinny path is a little rock tightrope. You can see it's been walked on, and the platform shows signs of wear, too, as if people were really dumb or suicidal enough to go there.

"Do it!" a girl shouts from the crowd.

So the bravest/dumbest/suicidal-est kid takes the shaky walk and a little leap at the end and lands on the platform, only just stopping his momentum without falling over the edge. Aunt Jodi watches this and just about has a heart attack on the spot. She can't stop herself from putting her hand to her heart and saying, "Jesus!"

The guy stands there and makes several goofy poses for his picture-taking friends. Now I get it. It's a photo-op spot. As if *every freaking inch here* isn't.

"Dude! Who's next?" the guy says, still copping poses for pictures.

He takes a good look at the run back before he does it. Measures it with his eyes and his feet. Finally, without warning, he takes three giant steps and then leaps toward his friends and barely makes it. He lands right at the edge, and one foot slips a little into the canyon. Dave jogs over and offers a hand in case he needs help. His friends are frozen, staring. The guy gets his footing, stands up and brushes the red dirt off his hands.

"You okay?" Dave asks.

"Never been better," the guy answers.

Macho jerk. He reminds me of Nader. Impressing his friends. Being cool.

The minute he's safe one of his friends does the same thing—and nearly loses his balance on the skinny walkway. He does that arm-circling thing that tightrope walkers do to stay balanced. When he gets back, his other friend goes.

Jodi looks at me watching them and has a worried look in her eyes, as if I might be thinking of doing it, too, but those guys look like idiots to me. I was never someone who deserved one of Aunt Jodi's worried looks, really.

The ants say: *Until the banana.*

I look down. I think about how one little second could change my whole life. How one false step could end everything I have. I ask myself if there was ever a time in my life that I'd do it—just jump. I think back to when I was seven, when Nader peed on my feet, and back to the time he punched me all year. Maybe then. Maybe if I was standing on the edge of the beautiful, enormous, amazing Grand Canyon right then, I'd have done it. I was little. It might have seemed a good solution. A way out. But something is different now. The world is bigger or something. My life is bigger.

The students leave in their rented Jeeps, and we're alone by the edge of the canyon. I'm leaning into the cool fencing over this one area, looking down. Mom stands next to me and looks down, too. She says, "Can I get a picture of you?"

"Sure."

She backs up and centers me in the viewfinder and says, "Smile."

But I don't.

On our drive back to Tempe, I make Mom and Dave talk a little about their mother. Mom tells a story about when Dave got suspended for hitting some guy named Alfred, and how their mom beat him out of the house with a broom and told him to sit on the porch until he grew up.

"She kept coming out to see if I'd grown up," Dave says. "Each time she'd go back inside and tell me I needed more time. She made me sleep there, too."

"I remember that," Mom says.

"If you ask me, Dave still needs more time," Jodi says, but while the others laugh, she doesn't laugh.

We stop for dinner in Flagstaff, and by the time we get home, I'm too tired to go looking for Ginny at the playground. As I fall asleep, I imagine Uncle Dave as my father again, and I try to figure out what the opposite of a turtle is.

RESCUE MISSION #108—JUNGLE PRISON COOK SING-ALONG

On the wooden chopping board are five ingredients. All high protein—a hawksbill turtle, a leatherback, a green turtle, a Vietnamese pond turtle and a Cantor's giant soft-shelled turtle. We are in Jodi's kitchen, at the breakfast bar, and Granddad sits on one of two stools, with his napkin on his lap. Limb report: all present.

I begin to separate the turtles from their shells and gut them while Granddad sings turtle facts to me, to the tunes of patriotic marches. First, Sousa's "The Stars and Stripes Forever":

"THAT POND TURTLE IS PRETTY MUCH EXTINCT.
YOU REALLY SHOULDN'T HAVE HIM OR EAT HIM.
THE HAWKSBILL IS EQUALLY ENDANGERED,
THANKS TO FISHERMEN WHO DON'T GIVE A SHIT.

"THE LEATHERBACK IS THE NEXT-BIGGEST REPTILE
AFTER CROCODILES AND DOESN'T HAVE A HARD SHELL.
THE GREEN SEA TURTLE SEEMS TO BE ABUNDANT,
BUT IT'S NOT, AND IT NEEDS THE SAME PROTECTION."

Then to Sousa's "US Field Artillery" (also known as "The Army Song"):

"THE MOST INTERESTING TURTLE
YOU'VE GOT HERE ON YOUR PLATE
IS THE CANTOR'S GIANT SOFT-SHELLED TURTLE.
WHAT OTHER CREATURE
CAN SIT COMPLETELY STILL
FOR NINETY-FIVE PERCENT OF ITS LIFE?

"HE'S MASTER OF THE AMBUSH,
CARNIVOROUS AND FAST —
NOT TO MENTION THAT HE'S SIX FEET LONG.
HE COMES TO THE SURFACE

"Sounds like Dad," I say, chopping the meat into long slices. Granddad doesn't say anything.

"Don't feel bad. It's not your fault," I add. I begin to fry the meat with garlic and chopped onion and some olive oil, and open the fridge to see what else I have. When I open it, all I see are flour tortillas. Hundreds of packages of flour tortillas. "I hope enchiladas are good with you."

"How can I not feel bad? I cheated you out of a good life with a good father," he says.

"Bullshit," I say. "You didn't cheat me out of anything. You're a hero. And Dad's old enough to know he can control his own destiny. If he wanted to be there for me, he would be."

"Looks like you're meeting him halfway."

I look at him—a salivating, wrinkled old man with eyes as big as the moon because the rest of his body has shrunk. "What?"

"This cooking you're doing. You've found the one way to reach him."

I turn my frying turtle strips over, noting the sour color of the meat—and the toughness. No matter what I add to these enchiladas, they will probably taste pretty bad.

"But Dad's a turtle, Granddad. Technically, we're about to eat him."

"Oh," he says. "I see."

The ants say: *Nom nom nom nom nom.*

When the meat is done frying and I've covered it in enough

chili powder to block out the brine, I throw it into flour tortillas and smother it in Monterey Jack cheese, and I serve it with a sauce I make out of the pan juices. It is probably one of the most disgusting things I've ever eaten. Granddad smiles and says, "Mind over matter, son. Smile and swallow. That's what I do."

• • •

I wake up with a horrible briny taste in my mouth. Not just the turtle enchiladas, either. I wake up tasting the reality enchilada, which I am not ready to taste, but I can't stop it from happening.

REALITY ENCHILADAS

1 cup of not really knowing if I can ever rescue
    Granddad
¼ cup of maybe Granny Janice was really high on
    morphine when she said that to me
1 tablespoon of ground squid 'n' turtle
4 cups of my real life sucks
2 cups of me not wanting to leave the jungle
    because I like myself there
a dash of maybe that's why I haven't rescued Grand-
    dad yet

Mix ingredients in bowl. Wrap in tortillas. Smile
and swallow.

OPERATION DON'T SMILE
EVER — FRESHMAN YEAR

We'd moved on from graphs and statistics in social studies class and had spent the last week studying the caste system of India. I still had a monthly meeting with the guidance department, and I still frowned the whole way through. I told no one about the questionnaires I kept finding in my locker, but I had a stack of about fifty now, which to me proved that I was not the only one in Freddy High who had explored the subject of suicide — making the guidance meetings more ironic.

Confusing a lighthearted teenage joke survey about suicide with something so serious really bothered me. Depression, the real thing, is a serious disorder. Suicide is a real thing that happens all the time. Somewhere out there in Freddy High, some students *were* really depressed. Somewhere out there in Freddy High, someone really *was* thinking about ending it all because of the bullshit they had to endure every day. I had proof that this was true—only I couldn't tell which completed questionnaires were serious and which weren't.

On a positive note, Nader was leaving me alone because he and his asshole posse were busy bugging other people, I guess. (Well, that and I'd pretty much learned how to completely avoid seeing him during the school day.) I heard they'd made sexually harassing Charlotte Dent into a sport. Rumor had it that a bunch of boys had rushed her during a postseason wrestling tournament and had a gang grope. There were other rumors, too—of worse things—but I didn't know what to believe. Charlotte and I didn't share any classes because she was a junior, but I saw her around the school and she looked fine to me. She smiled a lot.

But occasionally her curlicue handwriting would show up on a questionnaire in my locker, and I was starting to believe she was serious.

If you were going to commit suicide, what method would you choose? She answered: *I'd slit my wrists, but only after duct-taping a garbage bag over Nader McMillan's big, ugly head.*

We had rules now about this kind of thing. If anyone threatened to kill another student, we were supposed to report it, because these sorts of thoughts lead to school shootings. But Charlotte Dent put me in an impossible spot. First, I wasn't supposed to ever mention my first social studies project again. Ever. It would only make things worse for me. Second, I had a hunch that Charlotte was only sharing this with me because she knew Nader had bullied me, too. So I was her one safe place to go, even if it was just through a slot in my locker. And third, I wanted to protect her. I didn't want her bombarded with the same school-district bullshit I was going through.

Something told me that whatever he was doing to her was probably just as hard to talk about as what I saw him do with the banana in the locker room.

.

LUCKY LINDERMAN *COULD* BE
STALKER MATERIAL

I'm an obsessed moron. I look through as many of Jodi's magazines as I can to find pictures of Ginny, and I stare at them. In one of them she's holding hands with this model guy, and he's all perfect-haired and stuff, and I feel jealous — even though I know he's just some model and she's not really holding his hand in real life.

I look up the Clemenses' number in the phone book, but it's not there. I am so close to asking Jodi if she knows it — or if I can use her ancient computer to Google their address, or the shampoo company so I can see more pictures, or this vagina play that she's doing — that I am starting to be scared that I'm stalker material. Seriously.

I have to stop myself and turn on the TV for distraction. I watch six back-to-back episodes of *SpongeBob SquarePants* until Dave shows up and produces a DVD from his briefcase, claiming that every pair of bonding males should watch *Caddyshack* together just once.

"If this doesn't make you smile, I don't know what will!" he says when he puts the DVD into the player. I feel instantly paranoid again that his interest in me is all a show. The ants say: *Just shut up and enjoy* Caddyshack.

On Sunday, Mom and I wake up at the same time. It's early — six thirty. Mom says she doesn't want to go to church today, and I'm really wishy-washy because I know going to church will mean I can see Ginny again, so I say, "I think we should go. I mean, they just took us to the Grand Canyon, and we owe it to them, right?"

Mom grunts.

"Anyway, it's not like Jodi is dragging us there to convert us. She doesn't even say grace or anything religious."

Mom grunts again.

"If you want, I can tell them that you're not feeling good. You can skip it."

She turns onto her side and looks at me. "Are you okay?" she asks.

"Yeah."

"Why the sudden interest in church?"

"I was just trying to help you out. Forget it. I don't have to go if you don't want me to."

She lies on her back again and thinks for a while.

"You're right," she says. "We owe them."

"And it's only church," I say.

Dave lets me borrow his pants again, and we head off in Jodi's SUV. The youth choir isn't singing today, and Ginny is in the second pew with her parents. I stare at the back of her head for the entire service.

When it's over, Jodi grabs Dave's hand and makes a beeline for them. As the congregation makes its way toward the front door, where the pastor is, she blocks the aisle and makes small talk.

"We took our houseguests to the Grand Canyon this week."

Ginny's mom says, "That's nice. Did you enjoy it?" The question is aimed at Mom, but Mom is zoning out, looking at the stained glass, so I answer for her.

"It was pretty amazing," I say.

"Dave and I had a nice romantic vacation," Jodi says, squeezing Dave's hand.

"That's great," Ginny's mom says. She has huge diamond rings and takes a second to look at them while Jodi talks about the view and the walking she did with Mom.

I smile at Ginny and say hi. She shifts to her left and looks at me as if we've never met. As if she never made me say "vagina." The ants ask: *What's* her *problem?*

"If you'll excuse us," Ginny's dad says as he steps past Jodi and Dave and shimmies up the aisle. "We have quite a busy day planned." I watch Ginny follow him, and as she walks by, she avoids eye contact completely.

For lunch we go to Jodi's favorite after-church diner, which is packed, and when we get home Dave asks me if I want to lift. I don't feel like it, so I say no.

"You're not going to start slacking on me, are you?"

"Just need a day off," I say. "I ate too much." I toss myself on the couch with *Catch-22* and open it up. All I can do as I turn the pages is think about Ginny and why she gave me such a weird look.

Jodi arrives on the opposite couch halfway through the afternoon, seeming bored. I glance up at her. She's staring at me probingly again. "Wanna make dinner again tonight?" she asks.

"I'm still stuffed from lunch," I say.

She sits and stares at me for another thirty seconds. "Wanna talk?"

I do not want to talk. But talking to Dave hasn't been so bad, and Jodi's been relatively sane for the last few days, so I shrug and say, "Whatever. Sure."

"I think you're a good kid," she says. "But you don't smile and you read too much."

Oh. She didn't mean talk. She meant: *Wanna hear me tell you what's wrong with you?*

And what the hell? Who tells a kid that he reads too much?

"I think your mom and dad wouldn't fight so much if you stayed out of trouble."

"I'm not in trouble," I say.

"That's not what your mother tells me. She says you got in big trouble last year for some project you did. Said you wanted to kill yourself."

"That's not what happened," I say. Why would Mom think Aunt Jodi would ever understand?

"Well, what *did* happen?"

"I don't really want to talk about it. But you have it wrong."

"So what happened to your face?"

"Some kid beat me up. That's all." I open my book and look at the words to give her a hint.

"So your parents sent you here."

"No," I say. "You have *that* wrong, too." I take a deep breath and exhale. "Look, they fight all the time. So she left because of him, not because of me."

"Maybe that's how you see it, Lucky, but that's not really what's going on."

The ants are lying in prone position on the coffee table, shooting tiny M16s at Aunt Jodi.

"Can we stop talking now?" I ask.

"Sure. Just know that I'm always here for you, okay?"

I skip dinner and go to bed early just to forget she ever said this to me. But I can't. Maybe she's right. Maybe I'm looking at it all wrong. Maybe it *is* my fault, even though I didn't ask for any of this shit to happen. I didn't ask for Nader to target me. I didn't ask for the school district to save me. I surely didn't ask for my parents to argue about the solutions. And yet it's my problem. All mine. And maybe that's why we're here.

As I fall asleep, I think about Ginny and the look she gave me at church, and it makes me feel that familiar sinking in my gut — the way I've felt every time I've seen Nader McMillan in the hall since I was seven. He didn't even need to say anything to me. Just his existence would make me feel powerless and stupid.

The difference, I guess, is that he gained his power by humiliating me. Turns out, when someone you actually give a shit about turns on you, it's even more powerful.

THE TENTH THING YOU NEED TO
KNOW—THE PILLS ARE NOT WORKING

I wake up to the noise of a vacuum cleaner again. Right outside our door. I hear the whir of it retreating, the whir of its attack, and then, *bam*, it hits the door. I am guessing Aunt Jodi took an aggressive vacuuming pill this morning. Mom sits on her bed, head in her hands, and mutters, "What was I thinking, bringing us here?"

"One day we'll laugh about this," I say.

"I don't know." She sighs. "I think it was a big mistake."

I sit up. "I don't know. I think it's been okay, mostly," I say. This makes her smile.

For breakfast Jodi has made a homemade crumb cake, which she claims was inspired by "Chef Lucky," and she insists we all sit down together to eat it. She says, "Families who eat together are stronger." Mom raises her eyebrows at me when Jodi isn't looking.

Then the phone rings. It's Dad. I am reminded that we do not have a strong family, no matter how much we eat together. Maybe Jodi is right. Maybe Mom and Dad are really having bad marital problems. I realize how little I know about their world, even though I live inside of it.

Jodi and Dave have cordless phones, but when Mom goes to talk to Dad privately in the guest room, Jodi says, "Lori, don't go too far. I don't want to be gossiped about in my own house." She points to the living room, with a suggestive *sit there* hand. Mom pretends she hasn't heard this and walks into the guest room and closes and locks the door firmly behind her.

Until Jodi started to throw a fit, I thought she was just being paranoid. Now, since she's thrown a spatula on the floor and stormed over to the guest room door and jostled the locked doorknob, I realize that things are getting out of hand. When I see her take a run at the door shoulder first, I reach out my hand to snap her out of it.

"Aunt Jodi! Stop!"

She runs for the door and tries to break it down like they do in detective shows. It bounces her back but doesn't budge. She tries it a few more times and then gives up and sits at the dining room table next to me and rests her face in her hands.

My mother quietly opens the door and looks over at me and then at Jodi.

Jodi says, "I'm sorry. It's my nerves. I'm all over the place today." She gets up and goes to her bedroom and closes the door.

I try to pass the time until Dave gets home by reading and doing a few laps in the pool between card games with Mom. Jodi has locked herself in her room, and Mom and I take turns listening at the door for sobs or footsteps, making sure she hasn't overdosed.

When Dave gets home, we go out to the garage to lift. After fifteen minutes of manly silence, he points out that my arms look more defined in just a week. "Another few weeks of working out and you'll have guns like these." He flexes and admires his biceps.

"I think it'll take more than a few weeks," I say.

"Well, you know, it's not all about the muscles. It's about the confidence, man."

"Yeah."

"Don't you feel more confident already?"

"Kinda."

"Kinda? Work with me here! You're a cute kid with defined arms. The girls will faint over you. I'm serious." I know he's exaggerating, but the image of Freddy girls fainting over me makes me laugh. I think of Lara and how she's probably forgotten all about me already and I've only been gone two weeks.

He stops doing curls and looks at me. "Really — you don't feel like you could kick that kid's ass now? Or at least stand up to him while he kicks yours?"

"Not really."

"Why not?"

I sigh. "Because it's not about kicking his ass. It's about getting away from him. Getting away from *all* assholes. I don't want to become one — I just want to escape them."

"Good luck with that. Escaping assholes is about as easy as escaping oxygen."

The door opens. It's Aunt Jodi.

"Dinner in five."

"'Kay."

"Don't come in all sweaty."

"'Kay."

When she closes the door, we look at each other uncomfortably, towel off, and cool down with a few stretches. I think back to the last thing Dave said to me and try to imagine what escaping oxygen would look like. It looks a lot like drowning.

An hour after dinner I claim time to myself to walk the development. Before the door shuts behind me, Jodi says, "Don't get lost this time!" in a perky voice that makes me want to scream. Her moods are rubbing off on me. One minute I feel sorry for her, the next minute I want to tell her to go die. The ants toss tiny grenades at her before I close the door and duck and cover on the front stoop.

Of course I walk to the playground. Of course it's empty.

Of course I sit there for nearly a whole hour, squinting into the darkness for Ginny. Of course she only shows up while I'm walking home.

"Hey," I say.

"Hey. You ready to go?"

I didn't expect this after the whole church blow-off. I still feel that hole in the pit of my gut and a need to protect myself. "Can't. Need to go home."

"Home? Like, Pennsylvania?"

"No. Like, to my aunt's house."

"Crazy Jodi?"

I nod. I am simultaneously embarrassed for Jodi and relieved. I'm so glad other people know she's crazy. Ginny pulls on my sleeve and gets me to walk with her toward the playground.

"You know about that?" I ask.

"About her being completely nuts?"

"Yeah."

"Didn't you see her in church with my parents? She's a passive-aggressive bulldog."

"Yeah. I noticed that."

She twists her hair to the side to stop the wisps from blowing into her face in the evening breeze. "She freaked out two years ago during Sunday service. Stood up and said all sorts of crazy shit."

"Like what?"

"Stuff about the people there. How everyone was just faking it. How none of us practiced what we preached. We were all hypocrites. That kind of thing."

"During church?"

"Yep. Right in the middle of the sermon. Just stood up and started yelling."

I take a minute to imagine this. Not hard to picture, since only this morning I watched Jodi run at a locked door in order to break it down. I have to say, when I picture her standing up and freaking out in church, I wish I'd been there. I might have applauded.

"She's on a lot of pills," I say. "Too many."

"Is she? Huh."

"Like, way too many," I say. "Kinda makes me want to get Dave to take her to a place to help her. She's that bad."

"Dave?"

"My uncle? I mean, you guys have treatment centers for stuff like that, right?"

She looks at me and narrows her eyes.

"What?"

She looks at me again, this time shaking her head a little and raising her eyebrows.

"What?" I ask again.

"You know she's probably like this because Dave fools around, right?"

It's as if she just kicked me in the nads. Sure, Jodi and Dave are not the warmest couple I've ever met, but they seem to have an okay marriage.

"A lot, too," she adds. "He has a bunch of girlfriends."

"No way," I say. Because no way, right? No way the only guy who ever seemed normal to me is really a jerk who cheats on his wife, right?

"Yeah way. Like—everyone knows this. News flash, dude."

"But—"

"But what? He works hard? He's extra sweet to her at home?"

"I —"

"You want to know how I know?"

"You said everyone knows."

"Yeah, but do you want to know how *I* knew before *they* did?" she asks, climbing the fence into the pitch-dark playground and heading past the swings, toward the little bus shelter on the other side of the road.

We cross under the amber streetlights and she sits on the warm sidewalk rather than the bench in the bus shelter. I follow her lead because I figure she knows something I don't know. She suddenly doesn't seem at all like a girl I'm falling inexplicably in love with after knowing her for one night. She seems like an older sister or a Seeing Eye dog.

She lights a cigarette. "I know because he used to screw my mom."

"Oh," I say. "Wow." I feel my chest tighten with this news. "That's heavy."

"Not really, when it comes to my mom. She's the exact opposite of everything she stands for."

"Oh."

"Huh. So you really didn't know?"

I shake my head.

"Where'd you think he went all the time? Work?"

I nod. I realize I got that idea from Mom when she told me that her brother was a workaholic, like Dad. *Not quite, Mom.*

She says, "What I can't figure out is which came first. I

mean, did Jodi go crazy *because* Dave is like that, or is that *why* he started looking elsewhere? You know?"

I have thought this a million times about my mother. Was she a squid when Dad married her, or has being married to a menu-obsessed turtle done this to her? Or was it the other way around? Did being married to a squid make my father into a workaholic turtle so he could avoid watching her go crazy, lap by lap?

"And I don't mean to be a bitch, but how Dave could ever go to bed with Jodi is beyond me," she says.

Fact is, I do not want to be picturing my aunt Jodi and uncle Dave having sex. I do not want to be drawing parallels to Mom and Dad. I do not want to think about any of it. Most kids my age are dying to be adults and do adult things, but not me. Not right now.

"Mom says he's great in bed," she says. "I mean, she says that to her friends. Not me. She doesn't know I know."

Seriously. I'd rather watch *Barney & Friends* with a sippy cup of juice and a plastic bowl of animal crackers.

She drags the last pull on her cigarette. "I can see him as a great lover. He's pretty hot."

"Okay, okay," I say, my hand out. "I get it."

She laughs and squeezes my thigh. "Does it run in the family?"

The bus comes to a stop in front of the bus shelter. I get up to walk toward the dark playground, and Ginny grabs my sleeve again, this time stretching it as she pulls me hard toward the bus. "I don't have any money," I say.

She puts a few quarters into the machine in front of the driver and yanks me into the bus.

"Where are we going?" I ask.

She doesn't answer.

Ten minutes later she drags me off the bus the same way she dragged me on. The right sleeve of my shirt now looks three inches longer than the left.

We get off at a stop that seems to be in the middle of nowhere. I hear highway traffic nearby, but there are no houses or businesses or anything. Just a bus stop and a skinny road with very few streetlights.

"This way," she says, walking toward the sound of traffic.

We walk for a while. I want to ask her why she blew me off in church, but I can't figure out how. I don't want her to turn on me and leave me on a strange road by myself. And I just want to keep feeling this nice, warm sensation of friendship. I realize that I've never felt this before.

The noise from the highway gets louder as we approach what looks like a knot of bridges — a mix of on and off ramps at different levels. The road we're walking on now is a municipal access road that continues under the ramp.

"Where are we going?" I ask.

"Be patient."

"I am being patient."

"Well, then be more patient."

We get to a brightly lit area where we can see the highway traffic racing by us. We walk for about a half mile in the valley of brown grass next to the road so no one can see us, and then she leads me to the shoulder of the highway and tells me to close my eyes.

I find I cannot do this.

She could push me out into traffic. She could be a horrible, mean girl who just feels like fucking with me, the way everybody else in my life does.

"Do it! Close them!"

I pretend to close my eyes, but really I'm squinting. The ants on my shoulders say: *We have your back, Linderman. We won't let her do anything psycho.* I squint anyway. She puts her hands on my shoulders and turns me around to face the opposite direction.

"Open."

"Holy shit," I say when I open my eyes.

I see Ginny, twenty feet high by forty feet wide, on a billboard. Her hair is fantastic, and her smile is a little flirtatious. There's no doubt grown men on their way to work are smiling because of this billboard. Even though they shouldn't be looking like that at seventeen-year-old girls.

She stands with her arms crossed, looking at it.

"You're famous," I say.

"I guess."

"What do you mean, you guess?" I point. "There you are. On a billboard. You're famous."

"For my hair."

"And?"

"And frankly, I'd rather be famous for something I *did*. Or my radical views on politics or my ability to sing high notes or understand physics homework."

"Huh."

"I know I should be happy," she says. "It's my first billboard. Fourteen cities, too."

"So why aren't you?"

"I don't know."

We stare at it for a few more minutes and then walk back down the shoulder to the municipal access road and the bus stop, and as we near it the bus comes, and we have to run to catch it.

"So?"

"So what?" I ask.

"So — uh — nothing, I guess."

She's sitting on her hands and rocking a little, like a kid. I say, "Your parents must be totally proud of you. You're a cover girl and have your face plastered twenty feet high on billboards and you sing solos in the choir and you do community theater. I mean, you're — really awesome."

"They don't know," she says.

"Oh," I say. "Well, they'll figure it out."

"No, they won't. They don't care about me, the person. Just me the money-making face they birthed."

"Really?"

She turns to me in the seat and says, "Every single day of my life has been planned out from the minute I wake up. When I was a kid, it was dance lessons and pageant schedules and auditions. I was a Gerber baby food kid — did you know

185

that?" I shake my head. "You know those sicko pageant parents who dress their kids up like grown-ups so they can win trophies for being pretty? That's my mom. Well, it *was* until my dance teacher told her I sucked."

"Huh." That's all I can say.

"Bitch told her I should take up another talent because my dancing was average. So the voice lessons started. And baton twirling and violin and flute and all the other shit I suck at."

"I heard you sing. You're good."

"Yeah. I'm okay, but I'm not the best. And my mother thinks that I should only compete with what's best. She took me out of the pageant circuit when I was ten. Since then she's been getting me jobs in random ads until the Favors from Nature thing took off."

"Does it make you a lot of money? I mean — if you don't mind me asking?"

"You mean *her*. I don't make anything. When we get checks, they are made out to her management company."

"Are they big?"

"They're okay, I think. She just bitches about how we'd make more money if I had a real talent. My dad is worse. He tried to send me to fat camp last year."

"*What?*"

"Said I should keep the pounds down since all I have going for me is my modeling."

I am slowly realizing that Ginny's parents are from the planet Wow, Really?

The ants weigh in: *I think you mean the planet Fucking Asshole.*

The bus drops us off, and we walk quietly and slowly as she smokes her cigarette.

"So are you gonna tell me who did that to your face one day, too? I mean, now that you know my whole life fucking story?"

"Maybe next time," I say.

"We have our last rehearsal on Wednesday, man. You want to come with us?"

"I do."

"Meet me on the swings at ten."

"Okay," I say. She reaches over to my shirt and gives it one last tug. This time she pulls me to her face and kisses me. It's a sister kiss. Platonic. On the cheek. On my scab. And in my brain, the scab begins to heal instantly. I smile nonstop the whole way home.

When I get to the house, the front door is unlocked, the lights are off and I am able to walk in and get into bed without anyone knowing or caring. Lying there, thinking about Ginny, I feel genuine joy — joy mixed with relief that she doesn't hate me the way she seemed to in church.

Then, just as I turn over to get some sleep, I realize I don't live here. Ginny isn't really my friend, and my real life sucks.

RESCUE MISSION #109 — OPERATION SNATCH BACK

It's me, Lara, Nader and Ronald — the guy with the red-tailed hawk tattoo — and we're all in jungle camouflage with M16s and shiny new combat boots, walking the worn path as if we own the place.

"Watch for booby traps," I say, and Nader makes some joke about boobies because even in my dreams Nader is a fucking asshole.

Lara puts her hand out—the signal for quiet. There are men ahead. They are walking our way, so we hide in the brush. As they get closer, we realize they're speaking English. I peek from under my helmet and see three white men, and one of them is Granddad Harry. There is only one guard in back—not Frankie—some younger guy with a hand-rolled cigarette. I give the whistle command to start Operation Snatch Back.

Nader grabs one guy, and Ronald grabs the other. Granddad Harry looks happy to see me and I push him to Lara as I wrestle the skinny young guard to the ground. He burns his face with the cigarette, and curses.

"Go," I say to the others.

"I'm not leaving here without you, Linderman," Ronald says.

I look up. Lara is nodding. Granddad is staring at her, smiling.

"Seriously. Go. I'll catch up in a sec."

The guard under me is struggling to breathe. I forget that in my dreams I am twice my weight. I am twice my strength. One quick move and I might break his rib with my knee.

The six of them are standing there waiting for me. I look into the eyes of the skinny guard. He's scared. Only then do I realize I can't kill him. I don't even want to. So I roll him over, tie his hands and feet together and leave him on the jungle floor.

I grab Granddad around the waist and help him run while Lara keeps a lookout behind us with her M16 at the ready. Ronald is up front carrying his guy over his left shoulder, strutting with his rifle in the other hand, scanning each inch of what's ahead.

We reach a clearing where there is a helicopter. We all hop in and take off. Nader is flying the chopper, and I am in the back making out with Lara.

Granddad and the other two prisoners are slumped together in the back, drinking water from our canteens. At first when I see him, I hesitate to continue making out with Lara. Then he winks.

"I know you think you belong here, but you don't," he says.

"I was sent here," I say.

"Why? To rescue me? You think you can really do that?"

I stare at him and his two buddies. Isn't that what I just did? Why is he asking me if I can do something I already did?

And then Nader steers the chopper directly toward a tree-covered mountain.

He screams, "See what happens when you fuck with me, Linderman?"

• • •

When I wake up, it's three in the morning, and I'm sitting up like when I was a kid, breathing heavily, crying a little and moaning. I'm still hugging my pillow-Lara.

Mom snaps me out of it by leaning out of her bed and putting her hand on my arm. "It was just a dream, Luck. Just a bad dream. Go back to sleep."

RESCUE MISSION #110 — OPERATION MASSACRE

This time it's only tattooed Ronald and me. Ronald is the perfect crazy Vietnam War character from any movie you've ever seen. In the dream, every time I look at him, he's laughing, or eating a big bug, or smoking three cigarettes at once, or killing an animal, or drinking pee or a gallon of whiskey, or doing something that isn't sane. Ronald is, without a doubt, the perfect person to take with me on Operation Massacre.

Because when we arrive at the prison camp, he opens fire on everything that moves, and kills everyone. Even Granddad Harry. And I think, "Well, at least we know for sure now."

LUCKY LINDERMAN KNOWS
MORE THAN HE LETS ON

I can't stop thinking about Uncle Dave. The truth about Uncle Dave. Uncle Dave, the town playboy. Uncle Dave, the guy who "knows women." Ugh.

I remember him telling me that he was a bully in high school, and I develop instant solidarity with Jodi. Yeah, she's kind of a basket case, but she doesn't deserve to be treated like this, either. Maybe we can be pen pals. I can send her recipes. I can love her. Anything to make up for what my uncle is doing.

I decide to make a killer lunch for her. I defrost chicken breasts and slice them into burger-sized fillets, and I call Aunt Jodi on her cell phone.

"Lucky?"

"Are you still at the store?" I ask.

"Yeah."

"Can you get me a chunk of brie and some cranberries?"

I can hear Aunt Jodi processing my question.

"Please?"

"What's brie?"

"Just go to the cheese counter and ask someone to point you toward the brie. It's soft cheese."

"And cranberries? Like — fresh ones?"

"Frozen is cool. They have those," I say. "Right next to the frozen peas."

I picture poor Aunt Jodi pushing her cart full of crappy frozen dinners to the gourmet cheese aisle and feeling all grossed out by the mold. But she succeeds. When she arrives home, it's nearly lunchtime and Mom is sitting at the table, reading a magazine. I've got three perfectly seasoned, grilled breasts of chicken ready for the final steps of our lunch.

"They smell good," Jodi says.

"This lunch is going to blow your mind," I say, taking the groceries she puts on the counter and loading them into the fridge.

"You thinking about being a chef like your dad?"

I shake my head. "I never cook at home."

"What time did you get in last night?" she asks.

"About midnight." I continue to stock the fridge.

She looks at Mom. "Did you know he was out so late?"

Mom nods.

I go back to hating Jodi for a minute, but then I remember that she probably asks Dave the same question every morning. *What time did you get in last night?*

"Are you ready to eat soon?" I ask, whisking up a very basic cranberry sauce.

"Sure. Give me ten minutes," Jodi says, and then she gets a glass of water and disappears into her room.

When she returns, I serve Mom and Jodi what I call a Lucky burger. Grilled, seasoned chicken breast smothered in melted brie with sweet cranberry crème sauce drizzled over it, topped with fresh lettuce, on a poppy-seed roll.

Jodi leans her head back to say, mouth full, "You really should be a chef, Lucky." When she says "should," a piece of lettuce flies out. "This is really good!"

Mom nods, and I think she simultaneously hopes I don't become a chef and turn out like Dad. The ants say: *Not all chefs have to be turtle chefs.*

Mom says, "So are you gonna tell us where you go at night, or what?"

"I just go for walks."

"And?"

"And that's it."

"Did you fall asleep on the playground again?"

"Sure. Yeah."

Aunt Jodi looks at Mom. Jodi says, "We heard you were on a bus with Virginia Clemens. That you two looked like an item."

I laugh at the "item" part, and I look around, nervous that all those weirdos from Wednesday morning are about to jump out of the hall closet and start asking me more questions about my bowel movements.

"We are *so* not an item," I say, grinning at the thought of it.

"But you were on a public bus with her?" Mom asks.

"Yeah. She said she wanted to show me something, so we went into town for an hour and then we came back."

"You know if her parents knew about this, they'd kill you," Aunt Jodi says. She adds, "And then they'd probably kill her, too."

"They sound like assholes," I say, which earns me a disapproving look from both my mom and Aunt Jodi as they chew their Lucky burgers. "All we did was walk for an hour. I'm like a little brother to her. Believe me. I have no idea what to do with a beautiful girl like Ginny."

Jodi looks as if she might argue for a second, then takes another bite of the burger. Mom is grinning a bit.

Jodi looks at Mom. "Do you mind if I ask him a personal question?"

Mom shrugs. The ants say: *Uh-oh.*

"Lucky," Jodi says, staring at me in that adult-who-needs-to-know-the-truth way, "have you had a sexual experience yet?"

I nearly spit out my mouthful of chicken. I chew and swallow and then wash it down with a sip of water. I don't know what to say, so I say, "You mean — uh — with — a girl?"

Jodi smiles uncomfortably. "Uh-huh. Yep."

"God, no. Like, at home I play cards with Lara at the pool and stuff, but I've never kissed her — or anybody, for that matter."

"You haven't kissed a girl yet?" She rests her chin on her hand in that daytime TV kind of way, and I figure that she's taken a Dr. Phil pill or something.

I shake my head, kinda proud. "Nope."

"Why not?"

I shrug and think about this for a minute. My scab reminds me it's there by sending an intense itch signal to my brain. The loose edges tickle my face every time I move.

"I think he's too busy in school," Mom offers as I chew and think.

I say, "I just haven't found a girl I want to kiss yet."

The two women nod and shake their heads in disbelief.

Jodi says, "I wish the boys around here thought like that. I hear a quarter of the junior class has an STD already."

"Ew."

"Yeah," Mom agrees.

"I just can't figure how this could happen, you know? Most of those kids go to church every Sunday and come from good families."

"But isn't that always what happens?" I say. "The kids who have the strictest parents end up being the ones who act out?"

After a minute, Jodi says, "Are you saying Virginia Clemens is having sex?"

"No."

"Are you sure?"

"Yes. Actually, I am. Not that it's any of your business."

Mom looks at me skeptically. "You've known this girl for a week and you know this type of personal information?"

I smile. "I'm a natural listener. What can I say?"

I think for a minute about what Aunt Jodi just said. "Are Ginny's parents extra strict or something?"

"They don't let her out of their sight—which was why I

was so surprised to hear that someone saw you two on the bus last night."

"She doesn't usually take the bus," I say.

"Oh?"

"Yeah—she usually sneaks around like a ninja. That's how I met her."

Mom has stopped eating and is staring at me. I can't tell if she thinks I'm cute or thinks I'm high or what. Jodi is staring at me, too. It's making me uncomfortable, so I start clearing the table and cleaning the kitchen while they finish.

But then I get this awful feeling that I've said too much. I go back to the table.

"You guys aren't going to tell, are you?"

Mom looks at me as if to say, "Tell who?" Jodi shakes her head and says, "If Mr. and Mrs. Clemens can't keep tabs on their daughter, it's not my job to tell them."

And right then I know that she knows.

It's the way she said "Mrs. Clemens." Flat. Emotionless. Hollow.

And I wonder if that's why she freaked out in church that time, and if that's why she goes every week. Does she go just to mark her territory? Just to show that she can?

Dave never shows up for dinner. He calls and says he's working late. My mother, upon hearing this news, probably pictures him chained to his drawing table, designing bridges. Jodi probably pictures him handcuffed to a bed somewhere in Tempe, being dominated by some leather-clad hooker. I don't really want to see him again.

THE ELEVENTH THING
YOU NEED TO KNOW

We spend Wednesday doing absolutely nothing. Mom swims. I nap. Jodi cheers for Dr. Phil. Fifteen days of living in someone else's house is exhausting. Especially if everyone thinks it's your fault.

After dinner I ask if I can go out, and I'm surprised when both women say yes. I don't tell them I'll be home late, even though I know the last rehearsal ran until after midnight. I stop in the bathroom to comb my hair, but once I do, I mess it up again because too-combed hair just doesn't look right on me. I lean in and carefully peel off the floppy edges of the scab, and when I'm done, it's the exact shape of Iowa. I rub in a little aloe but then wash it off in case it dries green, and then I put on a clean POW/MIA shirt and leave.

To my surprise, Ginny arrives at the playground early. She's in 100 percent ninja black and greets me with a salute.

"Hey," I say, and salute back. "You're early."

"Am I?" She threads her arm through mine and we walk elbow-locked toward the swing set. "I didn't know we had a set time."

I stutter out a goofy laugh. "Well, yeah, you said ten."

"I wanted to have some time to talk," she explains. "And I knew you'd be early."

"Oh, yeah," I say.

"So . . . are you gonna tell me about it?"

"About what?"

"About that scab on your face. About how you always wear those fucking shirts. About why you're here."

"You know why I'm here." We each sit on a swing. She produces and lights a cigarette.

"I only know what you told me. But I know you haven't told me everything, Lucky Linderman. Like, what's *really* up with your dad? Is he a control freak or something?" she asks.

"Not really," I say. Then, "I guess. About some stuff. He wouldn't talk to us if he didn't have to. I mean — it's not that he's a dick. It's just not in his nature to confront things."

"And that?" She points to my POW/MIA shirt.

"My grandfather is MIA since 1972 — that's my dad's father. Dad never met him, which is the primary reason he's a turtle, I think. My grandmother was a POW/MIA activist. She pretty much raised me until she died of cancer when I was seven. And my dad hasn't got over any of it — not the MIA stuff or the cancer stuff—so now he can't face anything other than work. Can't face me, can't face my mom—" I pause. "But I guess it isn't easy being married to a squid, either."

Ginny laughs. "Oh my God. I forgot she's a squid!"

Her laughter gives me an instant boner. I find myself watching her hair fall in front of her perfect face and shake up and down with her giggling body.

"So what really happened to your face?" she asks. "I mean, you don't just fly two thousand miles because you get beat up, right?"

I sigh.

I hear myself explain the scab, but it's sort of an out-of-body experience. It's like some other kid is explaining how Nader McMillan has bullied me since I was seven, when he peed on my feet. This other kid is explaining how Danny made me and Nader try to be friends in freshman year and how it backfired.

Some other kid is describing the freshman-year locker-room banana incident—how they held him down. How they chanted. How they blindfolded him and made him take it into his mouth and threatened to put it other places. How he puked. Repeatedly.

Some other kid's brain is making note of each accomplice and blurring Danny Hoffman's face like deep cleavage on TV.

Someone else is explaining how I helped Charlotte at the pool when Nader was trying to make her go topless. Someone else is explaining the moment he used my face as a scrub brush on the concrete next to the men's room, and how he called it karma.

I come back to my body. "You know, I think it was a wake-up call."

"Seriously? Because in my world that's assault, and you should have called the fuckin' cops," Ginny says.

"I have the weirdest memories of that minute," I say. "I remember the smell—the hot-sun-on-cement smell. The chlorine smell. But I don't remember the pain." I do not tell her about the ants, even though they are screaming: *Tell her about us!*

"Just so you know, that asshole is not your friend."

"Yeah, I know," I say.

"Seriously, Lucky. You need to hang out with friends who act like friends."

I nod.

"It'll probably leave a scar," she says.

"Yeah. I'll have one big white cheek forevermore. I know. Did you see it's the shape of Iowa now?"

She leans in and looks closely. "No shit."

"Cool, eh? Started out in the shape of Ohio."

"So did you like this Charlotte girl? Is that why he did it?"

"No."

"Do you like anyone? Like a girlfriend back home?"

"No."

"Really?"

"I have a friend Lara, but we just, uh, read books and play cards and shit. I mean, I *might* like her, but I can't tell." I feel a little choked up and shaky.

"Are you gay or something?"

"No! Are you?"

"Hey! I *have* a boyfriend," she says.

"You do?"

"Yeah."

"Oh. I didn't know that," I say, realizing right at that moment that Ginny is the only girl I've ever met who I want to kiss. She's the one. And she is seventeen and beautiful and she can say "vagina" and her boyfriend is probably equally beautiful and smart. I'm like a retarded monkey compared to them.

"How would you? I never talk about him."

"Why not?"

She refers to her black ninja outfit with her hands and says, "Hello? I live with freaks, remember?"

"So your parents wouldn't want you to have a nice boyfriend?"

"Not until I leave college."

I laugh. "College? Won't you be ancient by then?"

"Yep," she says, not laughing at all.

"Wow. I'm sorry you live with freaks."

"At least I don't live with a squid or a turtle. I can't imagine that's so easy, either."

"Actually, it's not that bad," I say. They would never send me to fat camp, anyway.

Ginny doesn't say anything.

"Is he from school?" I ask. "Your boyfriend?"

"No. He graduated."

"Oh, wow. I'd say your parents would stroke out if they knew."

"You have no idea."

After a few seconds of silence, I ask, "Can I ask a dumb-little-brother kind of question?"

"Sure."

"Isn't it hard to stay a virgin with an older boyfriend? I mean — don't you feel pressure?"

Ginny starts to laugh, and I begin to feel stupid for asking. "I'm *sooo* not a virgin, Lucky."

"Seriously?"

She nods. "Yeah — not since I was your age."

"But what about the others? In the car? Didn't you all say you were virgins?"

She sees that I'm feeling embarrassed, and puts her hand on my knee and squeezes. "We said that to make you feel better, man. But I think Annie might have been telling the truth. The others? No way. I was there when Shannon lost hers."

"Ew, really?"

"Well, I wasn't *in the room*, but I was nearby — at a party."

"Doesn't sound romantic to me," I say, patting my scab a little because it stings from embarrassment.

She gets serious and faces me. "Look at me." I'm looking at my shoes. She reaches to my chin and tips my head up to look at her. "Look at me, Lucky."

I look at her.

"A girl's first time is pretty much *never romantic*."

"Really?"

"Hell no, man. Are you kidding?" When she sees I'm not kidding, she adds, "Think about it. Imagine you and I were going to have sex right now. First of all, how romantic is the playground? Ew, right?"

"I'd take you somewhere else, you know, with a bed," I say, though this is getting a little too weird and I don't want to talk about it anymore.

"And?"

"And then it would be romantic," I say, trying to do that thing Dad does, that inflection that means *this is the last word and the conversation is over.*

"Oh my God, Lucky. You really haven't thought about this shit, have you?"

I don't say anything.

"Stop and really think about it," she says. "And then tell me what would make you so romantic compared to other guys." She looks at her watch and lights another cigarette. "Five minutes until our ride gets here. Do you want me to teach you how to kiss?"

"What?"

But before she can answer, she is kissing me, on the lips, forcing my teeth open with her tongue. I lean forward so far on the swing that I nearly fall off, and I have to grab the chains to stabilize myself. This is not a sister kiss. She caresses the back of my head and stops between each tongue kiss to lightly lick my top and bottom lips. I now have a boner that will never go away. Never ever.

She stops and takes a drag from her cigarette. "So — is it really like licking an ashtray?"

I say, "I'd say . . . no."

She gets up and paces in front of the swings. I stay seated. Of course.

"See how you were so caught up in that? See how you couldn't move your arms?" I nod. She's right. I couldn't. "That's what your first time is like. It's a crazy mix of fear and excitement and white noise and — uh — lust, I guess. It's *not* romantic."

"But that *was* romantic," I say.

"But that wasn't your first bonk. It was just one little kiss."

She may think that, but to me that was not just one little kiss. The ants say: *Pay attention, Mr. Romance. She's got a point.*

I think about it. "I *was* kinda paralyzed."

"Exactly. And you will be when you do it the first time. So don't put any high expectations on it. Just try to get through it without hurting anyone."

"Hurting anyone?"

"Yeah. Guys hate being out of control. And they hate emotions. And they hate feeling let down. So try not to take it out on the girl, 'kay?"

"I don't get it."

She takes a long drag off her cigarette and aims her ear to the sound of the approaching car. "Every asshole I know in school blames the girl after their first time — for it being a letdown. Guys don't think about what it's like for us."

"Oh. Okay."

"Seriously. You have to think about more than getting laid. Otherwise you get so caught up in the sex stuff you're, like, a date rapist or something, you know?"

I have no idea what to say to this, so I don't say a word.

"And don't think that kiss meant anything."

"No. Of course not."

"It didn't."

"I know. I —" Before I can say the rest of that sentence, she kisses me again. And I kiss her back.

Right then I know I am hopelessly in love with Ginny Clemens. Not in a real-world sense but in the same way I could be in love with a movie star. I am so glad I told her everything tonight — about my parents and the scab and even the banana incident.

Though I half lied about that, because I didn't tell her that the kid they blindfolded in the locker room was me.

And I didn't tell her that they took all my clothes and left me slumped naked and puke-covered in the corner of the locker room, sobbing.

And I didn't tell her someone took pictures with a cell phone.

And I didn't tell her that I nearly went home and shot myself that day with the gun Dad keeps on the shelf in his bedroom closet. How I would have, if only the gun had been loaded.

Because I couldn't face another day.

In the car Annie offers me her leftover Wendy's cheeseburger and fries. I say yes even though I'm not hungry. The girls talk about their play, *The Vagina Monologues*, and I am completely lost in their lingo.

"Shan, you need to up the tension more during the Bosnian part. Annie has the happy parts so hyped, we need you to be more intense and dark, you know?"

"And, Maya, you can't laugh during 'Crooked Braid.' You can't even smile."

Maya nods. "I know. I can't help it. I love that part of the story."

"I dig that, but you can't, okay?"

Maya says, "We got signs up all over ASU campus today. The girls in my dorm all say they're coming."

"I hope we pack the house, man," Karen says. "I want to make a shitload of cash for the crisis center."

"That's so cool," I say. "You donate the money?"

"That's the whole point," Ginny says. "The monologues are staged all over the world so people can raise money and help survivors in their communities and in other countries."

"Awesome," I say, and I think of her parents, who drag her to church, and how proud they should be that she's doing something to help others. I think of how she can't tell them. She's like a kindness ninja. Sneaking around in order to help people.

When we get to the rec center, the door is open, and a woman about Mom's age is there, reading through a three-ring notebook.

"You guys ready to rock this?"

In unison the girls answer, "Hell yes!"

"Who's this?" she asks, looking at me.

"I got Lucky," Ginny jokes.

I wave a little and introduce myself. "I'm Lucky — a friend of Ginny's."

She waves back. "I'm Jane."

She raises her eyebrows at Ginny, and Ginny shrugs.

I sit in a seat toward the back, where a few others are sitting, and I watch the girls ready their scripts and coordinate their lines, and then they do the show from beginning to end, and I am completely dumbstruck by *The Vagina Monologues*.

First off, it's about vaginas. I mean, obviously, right? But until I hear them talking about it, I've never really thought about vaginas like this. You know, the way I have a dick and I use it to pee all the time. Girls have vaginas, and they have all sorts of stuff to do with it. Periods and babies and sex and going to the gynecologist, which doesn't sound like a lot of fun, but in the show they make jokes about all of it and completely crack up.

But then it's about rape. And how vaginas are treated by men and soldiers and people who want power. There are these two parts where I'm crying, you know? Because these two girls are talking about how they were gang-raped by soldiers in Bosnia. And there's this other part about some guy who beats up his wife so bad she nearly dies. Heavy shit, but really good because these girls are making it real or something. And then after some horrible story about what's happening to girls and women in Congo, there's a moaning monologue. They all pretend to have orgasms in different ways—Jewish ones and Irish ones and overly theatrical ones (I didn't even know girls could *have* orgasms). And then they chant hilarious vagina slogans and make us laugh all over again. It's a roller coaster about vaginas—a fucking amazing roller coaster of *reality*.

It's the reality I've wished for every day of my bullshit life.

OPERATION DON'T SMILE
EVER—FRESHMAN YEAR

Toward the end of the school year, more questionnaires came into my locker. At this point I realized someone must have made copies, because there was no way my originals could have lasted this long.

The answers were consistent—*pills, car fumes, pills, drug overdose, gun to the head, pills, self-drowning.* (Which is one I just don't get. It seems too difficult to actually work.)

I was pulling a 102 percent in social studies class, and Mr. Potter and I were bonding in that student-teacher way in which he almost treated me like an adult.

One day after class I told him about the questionnaires.

"I know I wasn't supposed to continue collecting the data, but it's out of my control."

"Have you saved them?"

"Some."

I played down the seriousness of it. "I mean—these are probably pranks. I got a bunch about jerking off to death and stuff like that. I don't think anyone is serious."

He nodded, and I instantly regretted telling him. If he told Fish about this, I'd be in huge trouble all over again.

"You're not going to tell anyone, are you?"

"Not unless you think I should."

"Nah. I think it's just people trying to yank my chain."

A week later, Charlotte's handwriting appeared again. *If you were going to commit suicide, what method would you choose?* She answered: *I'd hang myself. Probably next week.*

I didn't sleep that night.

RESCUE MISSION #82— CHARLOTTE'S NOOSES

In front of Granddad's camp, there was a plywood structure, kind of like department-store dressing rooms. In each area there was a noose. Like gallows with privacy walls. We were hanging, but our hands were under our chins, so we weren't dying. In fact, we were talking to each other.

CHARLOTTE: I can't believe I'm going to die.
ME: You don't have to. You can pull your head out and jump down if you want.

CHARLOTTE: I brought this on myself.

ME: No, you didn't.

CHARLOTTE: I told my mom what happened. She told my dad. He said I shouldn't wear short skirts.

ME: That's stupid.

CHARLOTTE: But he had a point. He said, "You think a jury who hears that you dress like a slut will think different?"

ME: People are assholes.

CHARLOTTE: Yeah.

Granddad approached us then. He looked at the plywood gallows and climbed into the next stall, placed his head in the noose and his hands under his chin, to hang on.

GRANDDAD: What the hell is this about?

ME: I don't know. I think it's about the questionnaires I've been getting.

GRANDDAD: You thinking about killing yourself, son?

ME: No. But I think Charlotte is.

CHARLOTTE: Nah. I'm fine. Everyone thinks about this shit, don't they?

GRANDDAD: I have.

ME: Me too.

CHARLOTTE: But I'd never do it.

We all climbed down from our nooses. Granddad found a folding chair for Charlotte and handed her a glass of water. Then we went to the back of the plywood structure, and we pushed it down on its back. Granddad collected the nooses, and they hung over his arm the way an ironed shirt might.

"What are you going to do with those?" I asked.

"I'm going to rescue myself," he answered, and handed one to me.

"Oh, good," Charlotte said. "That's the best way to do it."

• • •

The last thing I wanted Mom and Dad to find under my bed after all the school-district bullshit was a noose, so I took it to school in a plastic shopping bag the next day to get rid of it. I was sitting on the bus in the morning trying to figure out the best trash can to stick it into, when Danny sat down next to me. Since the banana incident, Danny stayed in the back of the bus with the other cool people who hung out with Nader, so this was surprising.

"Nader's not done with you."

I ignored him.

"Did you hear me?"

"What's your fucking problem, Danny? It wasn't that big a deal."

"It got him in trouble."

"Yeah, well, it got me in fucking trouble, too, and if he doesn't watch himself, he's going to be in more trouble. Those rumors about him rushing girls are going to land him in jail if he's not careful."

He laughed. "It's not illegal. The only reason girls have tits is so we can grab 'em, right?"

What do you say to this? What do you say to an idiot who'd repeat anything Nader told him?

I said nothing.

That day was my monthly guidance meeting, and it took everything I had to not tell the guidance counselor about Charlotte's completed questionnaires. I did mention the groping rumors, though.

"Does it bother you?" the counselor asked.

"It bothers me that no one is doing anything about it," I said.

"Believe me, if we acted on every rumor that went around this place, we'd never have time to do our jobs."

LUCKY LINDERMAN DOESN'T
USE THE STUPID SHAMPOO

We're all stuffed in the car again, on our way back to the playground. The girls are totally stoked after a great rehearsal. The ants are standing on the dashboard in vagina formation. ({})

"The only thing left to solve is getting my ass out of the house on Friday for the show," Ginny says.

"I say you walk out in defiant protest of how lame your parents are," Maya says.

Ginny laughs. Karen, who's driving, says, "Leave a runaway note that says you ran off with your forty-year-old boyfriend who knocked you up."

They're all laughing now. Except me. I say, "Hold up. Your boyfriend is forty?"

Ginny smacks my arm. "No, stupid. She was kidding."

But it's too late. I can hear them all realizing it at the same time. I have totally busted myself.

"Jesus, Lucky. If I'd known you were so possessive, I never would have let you practice on me," Ginny says.

My heart breaks a little, and I can't talk while it does that.

"You let him practice?" one says.

"Ginny, you hussy!" another says.

"Did he fall in love?" another says, and everything blurs into an embarrassing thumping in my ears as the car erupts with laughter again. The ants march out the windows and jump to the roadside with their thumbs up. Even my scab wants to jump off my face and abandon me.

When I finally look away from the street, I face Ginny, who is twiddling her hair in her fingers and smiling at me. She winks and kisses the air. The streetlights reflect off her hair, and I remember who I'm looking at. The Favors from Nature girl. The "It's Only Natural" girl. Her confidence is lifelong and enormous, the way my lack of confidence is lifelong and enormous. I look at the other girls — they all have it. I am the only one who can't laugh at funny jokes about myself. I am the only one who can't face the truth about myself. I am the only one pretending.

And pretending leads here. It guarantees nervous sweating anytime anyone talks honestly and the unreasonable fear that someone will say something that's *true*. It guarantees that I won't be able to handle it. Even if it's supposed to be funny.

Ginny lowers her head and joke-pouts to get me to lighten up. Then her eyes go wide and she sits forward. "I've got it!" she says. "I've got it!"

The car goes quiet because we think she's going to say something else, but she doesn't.

Shannon says, "And?"

She's breathless. "I know how to get out."

"*And?*" the girls ask in unison.

Ginny mentally walks through her plan in silence.

"Come on! Dish!"

"It will ruin the surprise," she says.

"Lame," Karen says.

"Yeah, lame," Annie says. "How will we ever know if you did it? I mean — whatever it is."

"Oh, you'll know," Ginny says.

"Write it down and leave it in the car or something, and then we'll know."

"Nope."

"How about you tell *the boy*?" Karen suggests.

"You won't need *the boy* to tell you what I've done. It will be more than obvious."

Karen parks the car in the playground lot, and Ginny and I get out of the backseat.

When they're gone, Ginny lights a cigarette and plays with the flame on the match for a second before blowing it out.

"How do you sneak in at night?" I ask. "I mean — if your parents are so strict?"

"I have magical ways."

"No. Seriously."

"Seriously? I rely on the sleeping pills they're hooked on. By ten they are so far gone I could march the Frontier High marching band right through their bedroom playing 'On Broadway' and they wouldn't wake up."

"Wow."

"Yeah. I'm fortunate," she says. "How do you manage to get away from Crazy Jodi?"

"I'm not sure. She stopped caring after last week. Something my mom said to her, I think." I pause. "Or she could be waiting for me tonight with the SWAT team. You never can tell with Aunt Jodi."

She nods and smokes.

"So what's the big plan for Friday?" I ask.

She smiles. "Oh, it's genius," she says.

"Are you going to tell me?"

"Are you going to come to the show?"

"I hope so. I mean, I have to ask my mom. We're leaving that night."

"So why should I tell you, then?"

We walk in silence for about a minute. I send the ants on a special assignment into her brain to press the *blurt it out* button.

"I'm going to shave my head," she says.

I make an audible gasp. "No!"

She stops and stares at me. "What do you mean, no?"

"You can't!"

"Why the hell not?" She's too loud for me to feel comfortable. It's one in the morning, and we are mere feet from a house.

"Because you *can't*! It's—it's..."

"It's what? Too beautiful?"

"Yes!"

216

"Too important?" she asks.

"Yes!"

"Is it? Is it really *that* important? It's just fucking *hair*!"

I nod. I am trying to picture Ginny with no hair. A hairless ninja. No more swaying in the choir.

She throws up her hands. "Haven't you learned *anything*? There are women going through *hell*, and you're concerned about my *hair*? *I am not my hair!*"

"But the money you make," I say, trying to save face. "You can donate it to the cause or something, right?" I look around for the ants. Surely they want to tell me how stupid I am for saying that.

"I told you I don't get the money. Anyway—you're missing the point," she says flatly. "You're forgetting that, above all, this will piss off my parents. And *that* is what I need to do to get my freedom. They control me with my hair. They confine me to that billboard, as if I have no other potential," she explains. "I thought you'd understand, you know? After a life of dealing with a squid and a turtle. After a whole life being bullied by some gorilla with no brain. You understand freedom, don't you?"

I squint at Ginny and picture her with no hair. She would still be beautiful. Her nose would still be perky with freckles, and her eyes would still be intensely green. She would still be awesome. She would still be smart. She just wouldn't have much hair.

"You're right," I say. "I think you're completely right."

"You do?"

"I really do."

"Why?"

"Because you're not your hair. You're amazing, Ginny.

You're a one hundred percent amazing person." She looks down at her feet and I grab her hands. "The world should pay you just for being alive."

She laughs.

"I'm serious. People like you should be in charge. Of everything. You should be worshipped."

"Well, I *am* kinda worshipped, you know. Billboards and all that," she jokes.

"True."

We walk for a minute, and she reaches down to hold my hand. "You know those commercials? The ones where the models say, 'I deserve it'?"

"Yeah."

"The day we taped them" — her voice wobbles — "I had to say it over and over until they got enough tape. *I deserve it. I deserve it. I deserve it.* I feel like I'm selling my soul, you know? I have a great life and get pampered and spoiled because I happen to have beautiful hair, while people suffer *everywhere.*"

"But—" I try to say something, but she's crying now, and she puts her hand out to stop my talking.

"You know the me on those billboards? The shampoo-me? The magazine-me? She has no soul."

"Stop it. She has a soul," I say.

"Maybe she has a soul, but it's so controlled by other people she can't see it in there anymore."

"It's in there."

"But it's dirty. They ruined it."

I stop her and hold her by the shoulders. "Listen to me.

They may control what you do, but no one can pee on your soul without your permission."

She nods as if she knows exactly what I'm talking about and, wiping her eyes, adds, "And anyway, I don't even use the stupid shampoo."

I think that's the perfect way to explain how I feel about everything in the world. I don't even use the stupid shampoo.

I have spent a lifetime chasing an old man abandoned by people who didn't think he deserved to come home. I have spent my whole life living with a man who didn't think he deserved a father, and a woman who thought she didn't deserve a say in her own life. It's all trickled down to me.

I've spent a lifetime being pushed around by Nader McMillan because I didn't think I deserved any better. Because I thought someone else should do something to make it stop. But that will never happen, because everyone who could have stopped it uses the shampoo.

I hug Ginny.

I get that feeling back again — that love feeling — but it's more intense this time because she's still crying a little.

"As far as I'm concerned," she says, "I'm done being the cover girl for bullshit."

"Yeah," I say.

"As of Friday my life will be mine and not the man's," she says, and then she kisses me again, and I swear I see stars. Or ants dressed like stars. Or whatever the visual equivalent of love I can't have is.

I smile the goofiest smile my mouth has ever formed.

"You know, Lucky, you're a really cute kid when you smile."

"Yeah, I know."

The ants nod and make goofy smiles, and that makes me smile more.

"I think you should keep it up, man."

"Thanks, I will." I can barely pronounce the "w" because my grin is so tight.

We walk to the place where we split. She says, "Show's at seven on Friday. I can sneak you in the backstage door if you want."

"I hope I can make it," I say.

"You should at least come and say good-bye," she adds, and then puts up her hood and disappears into the backyards of Tempe.

I walk to Jodi and Dave's house, still smiling. The door is unlocked, and no one is waiting up, so I lock it behind me and tiptoe into the guest room, where I slip into bed and think about *The Vagina Monologues*, and I feel that roller coaster of reality again. I think of all the reality I'm about to face. Two days until I fly back to Pennsylvania, where my father lives. Where Nader McMillan lives. Remarkably, this doesn't kill my smile.

RESCUE MISSION #111—BANANAS

Nader McMillan is sitting in the corner, weeping. He rocks back and forth, barely hanging on to sanity. Good. I'm glad.

The small hut is filled with bananas. Heaps of them. Frankie, Granddad's guard, and his two young guard friends are sitting at a table smoking cigars and playing poker. Every time Frankie loses, which is every game because Frankie plays shitty poker, the two young guys get to do whatever they want to Nader McMillan.

Outside it rains frogs. Big, bouncy frogs that hit the thatched roof with such speed and force I am sure the hut will topple in another hour if the rain doesn't slow down. I am sure we will be up to our pits in frogs.

"Lucky," Nader whispers.

I ignore him.

"Lucky," he whispers again, this time sobbing after he says it. I look at him. He mouths, "Help me." I look away.

I am crazy with hatred for him. I know this. I am okay with it.

I point to the scab on my cheek. Before I had that scab, there was no scar from the banana incident. The only scar was on my brain. Now I have something I can point to. I have something that can be photographed. Teams of psychologists can line up the pictures and say, "Lucky Linderman's gone insane after receiving a blow to the cheek in the shape of Ohio/West Virginia/Michigan/Iowa." I point to the scab, but really Nader knows what I'm pointing at. The scar that will never heal. The scar shaped like Florida or California. My banana-shaped scar.

I mouth back, "Fuck you."

The ants march single file to his face and spell it out right on his greasy forehead: FUCK. YOU.

Granddad is on his mat, meditating.

He says, "You have to live in the present, Lucky."

"But it's impossible to forget."

"I didn't say you had to forget it. Never forget it. But stop living there. Live here, in the present. Think forward to your future."

"My future is three more years of Nader McMillan."

"Yes, but from now on you're the one in control."

When Frankie loses the hand and it's time to torture one of the prisoners, the young guards point to Granddad. Frankie points to Nader. "Young!" he says. "Brave!"

But they want Granddad.

I look away. Granddad doesn't even make a noise. He is happy to eat the banana after the ordeal is over.

Nader McMillan screams. The hut is awash in frogs. The door is forced open, and they rush in and begin to drown us.

Granddad and I flow quickly through the window and land on frog rapids, riding them with no boat. A minute later Granddad and I are on the muddy shore, his legs a mess of fractured bone, clots, yellow fatty stuff and other colorful sinew. Mine are inexplicably perfect — not even a scratch.

"How have you lived this long?" I ask.

"My time's not up, I guess."

"No, I mean, how do you survive this?"

"I just do," he says. "When they torture me, they show they're weak. When I survive, I show them I'm stronger."

"My life is mine," I say. "Not the man's."

"Exactly," he says while rearranging his tibia to line up with the rest of his leg. "You're stronger." He bends his knee a few times to make sure he's all fixed up. "Can I ask *you* a question?"

"Yeah."

"Why do you keep coming here?"

I can't understand why he's asking me this. It makes me angry that he has to.

"You know," I say.

"Tell me anyway."

I sigh. "I'm here to rescue you. To bring you back."

"Why?"

"Jesus! Because you shouldn't be here! You shouldn't be here!" I say. "And Granny Janice told me to. Because we need you."

"So you were sent here. That's why you're here?"

"Yeah."

"So what if I tell you to go away? Don't come back?"

"I wouldn't do it," I answer. "I have as much reason to be here as you do."

"Son? Do you really believe you can drag me out of this place through your dreams?"

I don't say anything. He pats me on the shoulder and hands me a stick of chewing gum that he pulls from his ear, as a magician would with a quarter. He produces a piece of gum from his other ear and unwraps it and pops it into his mouth.

"Think about it for me, will you?" he says.

• • •

When I wake up, I'm still smiling that goofy smile Ginny said was cute. And I'm holding a stick of chewing gum, and I think about it like he asked me to, but I don't really know what to think. Is he asking me to give up my life's mission? Or is he telling me that this *isn't* my life's mission?

THE TWELFTH THING YOU NEED TO KNOW—IRON PYRITE LOOKS A LOT LIKE GOLD

Mom, Jodi and I have been in the car for a half hour. Jodi drives too slowly and gets freaked out if anyone behind her gets too close.

"Get off my ass!" she says. "Oh! You want to play? Because I can go slower!"

Mom is watching the desert crawl by out the passenger's-side window and is probably dreaming of the laps she'll do when we get home. I'm lying across the backseat in case any of the people behind us decide to shoot Aunt Jodi for driving like a crazy person. You never know.

We pull into the dirt parking lot of an old gold-mining town—now a tourist attraction—and Jodi says, "Here we are!"

The three of us spend the next hour wandering the place,

even though it's more than a hundred degrees outside. Jodi gets a picture of me (sweating) behind the bars of the small-town jail. We sit and talk for a while with the sheriff, who totally notices that my scab is the shape of Iowa. Behind him, costumed floozies play poker. We have a root beer in the saloon and wait for the hourly gunfight to start. Though it's totally touristy and lame in ways, it does make me think about what this place must have been like back in 1890.

"Imagine that," Mom says.

"Yeah," I answer. "Crazy to think that's the way things were." Of course, things are still kinda the same. I mean, there are probably more shoot-outs now than there were then.

After the gunfight is over, we put a few bucks in the dona-tion hat and walk up to the brothel. Jodi, Mom and I stand outside while the faux hookers invite us in. We go to the black-smith next door instead. When we get to the top of the town, Jodi goes into the little white chapel while Mom and I sit down and share a bottle of water.

"You okay, Mom?"

"Sure."

"No. I mean, *are you okay? To go back?*" I ask.

She nods. "Can't wait to see your dad. I miss him."

"That's good," I say. I can't figure out what there is to miss, but that's between them.

"I hope you know I had to do this for myself. It wasn't really anything to do with you," she says. "I mean, it *does* have to do with you, but it's not your fault."

"I know." I say. I watch as the ants act out a gunfight with tiny pistols in the dirt at our feet. I envy how much fun they have sometimes.

"All those years..." She starts to cry a little. "I wanted to call the principal or the superintendent. Once, that time when you had the bruised nipples from the twisty-nipple things—"

"Titty twisters."

"Yeah." She shakes her head and bites on her bottom lip. "That time. I wanted to call the police, I was so mad."

"I heard that fight," I say.

"It's not that he wants you to suffer. He just doesn't know what to do about it, so he thinks there is nothing to do about it."

I nod.

"I mean, we tried! Remember that time we got him suspended?"

"The pencil," I say. Nader stabbed me in the arm with a pencil in fourth grade. After he came back from suspension, he punched me in the ear so hard I couldn't hear right for a week. His father threatened the school district. Said if Nader got "unfairly suspended" again, he'd sue.

"And then your father thought up *the plan*. Thought he was a genius."

The sun is baking us into human raisins. If Aunt Jodi docsn't hurry up, we will be two piles of dust.

"Reverse psychology, he told me. *Maybe if we don't say anything, they'll just leave him alone*. And I fell for it because I was sick of arguing." She looks at me, the direct sun making her face look older. "But look at everything you lost because I was sick of fighting with a stupid man over his stupid idea."

"It's okay, Mom."

"It's not okay. I'm your mother."

"Yeah, but I stopped telling you guys stuff a long time ago. I stopped telling anybody," I say. "Anyway, we're here now."

She looks at her watch and over toward the chapel. "We're here, all right. Why, I don't know. This was probably the worst place to bring you!"

"Not really. I feel better."

"Really?"

"Yeah. Dave taught me a bunch of stuff. And just meeting Jodi kinda showed me how normal my life is. I mean, even with Dad storming out a lot and wishing we were ham hocks."

We watch Jodi waddle from the door of the chapel, and I add, "I kinda like her, you know? She has redeeming qualities or something."

Mom chuckles and says, "Yeah. She has something. Not sure what."

Here is where I would tell her about Dave cheating if I had more time, but I don't. I don't want to ruin her relationship with her only sibling, or mess up anything more than it already is.

When Jodi returns, she says, "You two ready to pan for gold?" and we walk down to the panning shack and the three of us buy a pan of dirt to sift through. The woman gives us vials for our gold and some tweezers. Mom finds more gold than all of us. Jodi says she's only after garnets this time because she's come here enough that gold is boring to her. Unsurprisingly, I end up with a vial full of iron pyrite — fool's gold. Last week this would have made me feel stupid. Today it makes me laugh. And it reminds me of what Granddad said last night. Maybe I'm looking at things all wrong. Fact is, iron pyrite looks a lot like gold, and I wouldn't be the first person in the history of the world to have confused the two.

When we get home, it's three o'clock. I watch Mom swim laps. She says she can't stand the short pool much longer. "Makes me feel like a condor in a birdcage," she says. I tell her that I'm taking a walk, which is insane because it's a hundred and ten million degrees outside, but I see Ginny walking with some girls through the common area behind Jodi's house.

I cut through the backyard, and by the time I catch up with her, she's talking with three normal-looking girls (long, straight hair done just right and ironed preppy clothes) on the sidewalk. When she sees me, she excuses herself and walks over.

"You're still smiling," she says.

"Can't help it."

"You coming tomorrow?"

"I think so," I say. "Are you still gonna . . . ?" I point to my hair and raise my eyebrows to indicate the rest of my sentence: *shave your head?*

Just as she's about to answer, there's a loud whistle. She turns toward her house. When she does, her hair swings like a wide skirt. I will miss it.

"Shit. That's my mom."

"She calling you or a dog?"

I look over and see a woman on the porch of the nicest house on the block. She has one hand on her hip, another in her mouth to whistle again if necessary, and she's looking right at me. Right through me. Then she points to her watch frantically.

Before I can say anything else, Ginny is gone. She stops to say good-bye to her friends, and while she jogs to her house, I watch her transform into a completely different person. Even from behind I can tell that person would never talk to Lucky Linderman, let alone kiss him.

We wait until six thirty for Dave. Jodi tries calling him on his cell phone, but he doesn't answer. So we leave for their favorite restaurant without him.

He finally calls while we're eating our bread and says he can't make it.

"A last-minute meeting," Jodi says.

Mom looks disappointed. Before Jodi can comment, she says, "I really should have planned this better so we didn't come when he was so busy at work."

Jodi and I look at our plates and don't say anything.

I gorge myself. I even eat dessert — the house cheesecake with strawberries. When I get home, Mom starts doing our laundry, and I go straight to bed because I can't wait for Friday because Friday is the day we leave. Because Friday is the day I get to see Ginny one last time. I can't figure out which is better.

LUCKY LINDERMAN ARRIVES AT FRIDAY

I wake up to Mom stacking her clean clothing on her mattress. She's stripped the bed and has borrowed Jodi's laundry basket, which is waiting for my sheets, I presume, before she will take it to the laundry room and wash them for Jodi. She stacks the piles exactly four inches away from each other. Each piece of clothing is folded perfectly, like a department-store table display. I fall back asleep.

The shower goes off, and Mom arrives a few minutes later wrapped in a towel.

"Get up, Luck. I need to strip your bed."

"Sure." I say this, but I want to keep sleeping.

"Up," she says, making the motion with her arms.

So I get up and take a shower, and when I emerge, I see my bed is stripped and my clothes are neatly stacked on my mattress as if they were for resale at JCPenney. The POW/ MIA department of JCPenney, of course, where our heroes are never forgotten.

I comb my hair and check out my scab in the mirror. The edges have shed their ragged dried bits, and Iowa has morphed into Pennsylvania now — a near-perfect rectangle with a jagged eastern edge and a ridge of mountains through the middle. I find this fitting for the day we're flying home.

While Mom takes her final few laps in Jodi's pool, I try to find Ginny. I walk by her house twice, once going east and once going west, but it looks as though no one is home, and so I go to the empty playground and sit in the shade for a while thinking that tomorrow I'll be home again. I nearly feel all the confidence I have here in Arizona collapse just thinking about it. It's as if location is more important than I ever gave it credit for.

The last place I remember being happy was at Granny Janice's house before she got sick. Since first grade, school has made me a jittering coward. The pool was fine until Nader started working there two years ago. Now I hate it. And home is a disaster for a variety of reasons.

I picture Dad alone for the last three weeks — raising the flags, driving to work, driving home from work and lowering the flags. Something about this scene makes me want to cry. Everything about it. All these years I've been visiting Granddad while he can't. When he folds that POW/MIA flag every night, that's his father he's folding. It's all he's got. It's all he's ever had.

◎

I'm eating a late lunch at the kitchen table when I hear Uncle Dave park in the driveway. The ants say: *Hey! Look who decided to show up!*

Dave walks in and says, "I'm so glad I caught you! I thought you'd have left by now."

"Our flight isn't until late. It's a red-eye."

"My sister has always been early for everything," he says. "Plus, I thought you might be out saying good-bye to your mysterious friends."

"Nah."

He cocks his head. "Is something wrong?"

"Nope."

He can feel my disgust for him. I am purposely sending it.

"Sorry I didn't make it yesterday. It's been a killer week at the office."

"Sure it has," I say.

He shrugs and goes back to the garage door. "Want to lift a little before you go?"

"Nah. Already showered."

He stands there looking at me, and I look back at him. Eye to eye. He has no idea that I know he's cheated Aunt Jodi out of a happy life. Part of me wants him to know this. Part of me wants to tell him to shit or get off the pot. The ants want me to drop a twenty-pound weight on his dick.

"Okay, then," he says. "I'm going out to lift."

Just as he's about to open the door, I say, "I know you aren't always at work when you say you are."

He stops and turns to face me.

"I *know*," I say again.

He looks a mix of caught and hurt, and I don't say anything else, so he opens the door to the garage and closes it behind him.

As I'm rinsing my plate in the sink, Mom and Jodi come in, toweling off and chatting about calories. Apparently, Jodi thought calorie counting was a myth.

"But let me get this straight. If I eat less than fifteen hundred calories and exercise every day, then I'll lose weight?"

Mom nods. "That's the idea, yeah."

"Why didn't they teach us that in school?" She wraps her beach towel around her lower half and slips on an oversized T-shirt.

"I think they did," Mom says. "But it was boring then. You probably forgot."

"Yeah, well, back then I could eat whatever the heck I wanted and never gain a pound."

"And another —" Mom starts, but then there's a banging on the front door and someone rings the doorbell, like, four times in a row.

Jodi is startled. We are all startled, because there seems to be screaming or crying or — Ginny. As Aunt Jodi opens the door, Ginny falls into the house, a lump of sobbing, hands over her face — and nearly bald. I do the first thing that comes naturally. I hug her.

We stumble to the nearest love seat, and she continues to sob into my chest.

I make eye contact with Jodi and Mom, and they both

shrug. Eventually Jodi grabs a box of tissues and sits down on the couch on the other side of Ginny. I hand a tissue to Ginny, and she cleans up her face and then looks at me, and I see she has a huge red-purple mark around one eye — a shiner in the making.

"What happened to your hair?" Jodi asks, because she hasn't seen Ginny's eye yet, and Ginny puts her head back on my shoulder and cries again.

I'm speechless. Picture this: girl with a white scalp showing through an inch-long white-blond crew cut, with a welt the shape of New Jersey forming around her eye, the red-purple starting in around the edge, her face puffy with grief. The most beautiful girl I've ever seen in my life. She's wearing a pair of oversize sweatpants and a T-shirt. She smells like salt.

Ginny continues to cry in my arms, and Aunt Jodi rubs her back in circles. "Virginia? What's going on?"

And then Ginny looks over and Jodi sees her eye and she's speechless for a moment.

I manage to ask, "Who did that to you?"

She traces the welt on her face with her index finger.

"Who did this?" Jodi says.

Ginny looks at me and reaches up to my scab and feels it. I can see her searching for an answer, but she bursts into tears again, and Jodi rubs her back and puts on that concerned face. Not like during the interrogation two weeks ago, but like a genuine concerned face. Like she could imagine Ginny being her own daughter or something.

I hear the radio go off in the garage, which means Dave is cooling down. Mom is still standing where she was when the doorbell rang. Ginny is taking deep breaths, trying to get a grip on herself.

"Do you need me to call Karen or Shannon or anyone?" I ask. She takes a tissue and blows her nose a few times and wipes her face.

She nods in response to my question, and Jodi looks at me with raised eyebrows, looking for direction.

"What horrible reason did they have for cutting off your hair?" Jodi asks.

"I did it," Ginny says.

Jodi interrupts. "But, sweetheart, I —"

"I'm sick of being hair," she says. "That's all I ever was! Hair!"

I nod.

"I think it's really nice," Ginny says, feeling the crew cut she gave herself.

I feel it, too. I make a face as if to say: *It is quite nice.*

I feel Jodi getting impatient.

"My mom freaked out," Ginny says. "She said my career is over, my future is over, my life is over. She told me that maybe she and Dad were going to send me to some boarding school or something."

Jodi looks again at Ginny's eye. "So — who?"

. "She did," Ginny says. "I didn't know what to do. She never did that before."

Jodi nods.

"She kept hitting and hitting," Ginny says. "Her eyes were closed. She thought she was still aiming for my arm, I think. She was crying, too." She inspects her arm and it's also red-purple.

"Over your hair?" Mom says in the most judgmental voice she's got.

Ginny nods and sobs a little. Her lower lip curls down, and she brings her hands up to cover her face again.

Mom wraps her towel around her midriff and sits down on the love seat across from us. "If you don't mind my saying so, hitting your kid is against the law. I don't care how upset she was. What she did is wrong. Completely wrong."

Ginny cry-nods. She's in shock. I recognize the symptoms. (I almost see her dancing ants myself.) She can't even consider fighting something as big as her mother.

That's when Dave walks in.

The door slams accidentally because of the breeze, and we all stop what we're doing to look at him.

"What's going on here?" he asks.

Jodi and Mom stand up and move into place as shields. Dave wants to see who's on the love seat with me, and Ginny hides her face in my chest, so all that's showing is her crew cut. I don't know what Mom and Jodi do to keep him over by the garage door, but whatever it is, it distracts them all for just long enough.

Next thing I know, Ginny is pulling my sleeve and we're out the door and running full speed through her ninja tunnels, passing all the familiar walls and fences and family dogs, but in the daylight. And yet we're invisible. No one yells, "Hey, you pesky kids! Get off my lawn!" No dogs chase us — or even bark. We are flying.

We get to the playground, and Ginny takes me to the maintenance shed, where she reaches into the eaves and produces a pack of cigarettes with a book of matches shoved into the cellophane. She lights one and sits on the corner of the concrete pad of the shed. Her hands are shaking. I sit next to her, silently.

It's all happened so fast it's hard to process. I don't even know what time it is. I just know I feel better off than Ginny. I mean, yeah, her family has a big house and money, and she does all this cool stuff, and her face is plastered on billboards. *Billboards.* But even with her cool friends and her *Vagina Monologues*, she still has to go home to that house at night and be controlled by those people who want her to be something she's not. Makes having a conveniently absent turtle-father look appealing right about now. Makes me wish she had a squid for a mother, too.

I don't say any of this. I just scratch at the dirt with a small twig. Ginny doesn't say anything, either. While she smokes, she reaches up to her eye and feels around. I get the urge to feel it, too, so when she takes her hand away, I turn her toward me and I feel the edges of New Jersey. I kiss Hoboken and Atlantic City. I kiss Newark and Trenton. I kiss Camden, and then I follow the road west, over the Walt Whitman Bridge into Pennsylvania. And I kiss home.

◎

"I'm going to fucking kill her!" Karen yells, driving like a nut-case in the middle suicide lane to get past two old people in a Cadillac. Maya is crying. Annie is silent.

"I think you should get her ass arrested," Shannon says. "Teach her a lesson!"

I'm holding Ginny's hand, stroking her thumb with my thumb. I'm out of the shock bubble now and thinking straight. "We need ice," I say. "And Advil. Do we have time to stop at a drugstore?"

Ten minutes later, I'm jogging through the CVS parking lot, Ginny has a bag full of McDonald's ice on her eye, and we're on our way to the next town. Apparently, that's where the theater is. I realize Mom is going to freak until she knows I'm okay and we're still going to make our flight, so I call her on Karen's cell phone.

"What show?" she asks when I tell her I am going to one.

My brain stutters until I remember that Mom has a vagina, so she shouldn't mind my using the word. "*The Vagina Monologues,*" I say.

After a few seconds she answers, "Where is it?"

"Where are we going?" I ask Ginny.

"Is that your mom?"

"Yeah."

"Can't say."

I cover the phone to say something, but I don't know what to say. It's their show. They've worked for months. Even though I trust Mom, I know adults can't be trusted right now. I can't just barge in and ruin it now because I'm a mama's boy.

"Sorry. Can't say."

She tells me to be home before nine, and hangs up.

By the time the doors open at six thirty, Ginny's New Jersey is less swollen. Karen has taken a few pictures with her iPhone, "for evidence," she says. Ginny has her binder in front of her and goes over lines marked in pink highlighter, jotting notes in the margins. Jane is talking to the girl running the spotlight, and is making sure the chairs onstage are on the tape strips that mark where they should be. People start to wander in, and a low murmur takes over the room.

I wander to the balcony to people-watch. Some stop at the clothesline Jane put up this morning—a collection of pieces of clothing with messages written on them by past and present participants in the show. After ten minutes I wander down and read them, too. A shirt says WOMAN POWER! Another, BEHIND EVERY GREAT MAN IS A GREAT WOMAN WHO PUSHED HIM OUT OF HER VAGINA. A child's bathing suit says, in Sharpie marker, I WANTED TO BE AN OLYMPIC SWIMMER. INSTEAD, I BECAME A DRUG ADDICT. Along the crotch of the suit, it says HE STILL COACHES. MAYBE YOUR DAUGHTER. My stomach twists.

I concentrate on the more uplifting lingerie. There are three pieces. One says WILL YOU PLEASE ME? Another, I DON'T NEED A REASON TO WEAR THIS. And the last, as wide as it is long, so it would fit Aunt Jodi, says I AM PERFECT.

The crowd grows, and I feel a little weird about being male right now, so I tiptoe back up the stairs to the balcony. At the edge of the staircase, I see one last item hanging from the clothesline. It's a hairbrush. On the back it says I DESERVE MORE.

The house is packed. The lights go down, and the girls make their way onto the stage. There are no costumes or props or anything. Just chairs. The spotlight and the dark stage make everything look professionally done, and the girls don't miss a line. They chant the funny vagina chants, and they talk the harsh vagina realities, and I am sitting on the top step, knees to my face, occasionally wiping my tears on the stretched sleeve of my POW/MIA T-shirt. It's a little like the Grand Canyon — I don't think I could come up with words to describe it if I had to.

When it's over, I join the standing audience and applaud until my hands are sore. Each of the girls bows a little. Karen reaches up to Ginny's crew-cut head and rubs it while Ginny reaches up to inspect her shiner with her fingers. The ants throw tiny roses at the girls' feet.

I walk down the steps and the aisle and am about to sneak backstage when I feel a hand on my shoulder and I hear Mom's voice behind me. "You ready to go?"

I jump a little. "Yeah," I say. Before I can ask how she knew where I was, the ants show up, each of them reading tiny weekend entertainment sections of the newspaper.

"I'm parked out back," she says, and points to the door behind the stage.

"Oh."

"You have time to say good-bye, but make it quick." She points to her watch. I remember we're flying back home now. I try not to feel as devastated by this as I am.

We find Ginny and the girls, and I hug them all and

tell them that I loved their show. I tell them that I'll miss them.

Karen says, "Don't be a dick, okay?"

Maya: "Stay virginal, Lucky. Your time will come."

Shannon: "Love your vagina, man."

Annie: "Bye, Lucky."

Ginny grabs my hand, which makes Mom excuse herself and slip out the back door.

"I'll miss you, Lucky. I mean, even though I don't really know you."

How do I say it? How do you tell a person that she's changed you forever?

"I want you to stand up to that asshole, okay? Call the cops if you have to. You deserve to be treated with respect," she says. Instinctively, I touch the scab, which makes her touch her eye. It occurs to me that if we kissed now, we'd be like a folded map of America. My Pennsylvania scab next to her New Jersey black eye. I wonder, then, how many other kids could join in. Where are the Montanas and the Colorados? Where is Vermont? Florida? How many maps could we make?

I say, "I love you. I mean, in a big-sister kind of way."

She hugs me. "I know."

I kiss her on Cape May. "See ya."

"Remember," she says. "Friends act like friends."

I look to the other girls and know they will take care of Ginny. Then I go out the back door to the parking lot, where Mom is waiting for me in Jodi's SUV.

Once we get onto the highway back to Tempe, Mom says, "I'm proud of you."

I don't think she's ever said it that way before. Before now, she'd say it like I was a kid. When I did something cute or aced a test.

This time she said it like she was talking to a man.

It's a quiet ride home.

Dave was supposed to drive us to the airport, but he got called into "work" for an "emergency," so we call a taxi and say good-bye to Aunt Jodi.

She hugs Mom for a too-long amount of time and pats her on the shoulder a lot. "You two take care of yourselves. If you need us, call us, okay?"

Mom nods. Jodi turns to me, "Stay out of trouble, Lucky."

I smile and say, "Tell Dave thanks for teaching me how to lift weights."

"I will."

"Tell him he should bring you out to see us soon," Mom adds.

"Will do," Jodi says.

The ants say: *Lay off the pills, man.*

The taxi arrives, and as I pack our things into the trunk, I tell Jodi that I'll e-mail her a recipe once a week to try, and that I'll make sure they're easy. I can see in her eyes that she plans on gorging herself with processed popcorn shrimp the minute I leave, and the entire sending-recipes idea will be a waste of my time. I decide to do it anyway.

Mom and I wave from the backseat, and I feel a collective weight lift into the clear Arizona sky. Three weeks ago the trip sounded like a great idea. Two weeks ago it was the worst idea in the world. Today I know it was the best thing that ever happened to me. Probably for more reasons than I can see yet.

As we take off, I watch Arizona's lights disappear underneath the plane. Before the seat belt sign goes off, Mom is snoring lightly, head leaned slightly to the right. I can only think of Nader. A bead of sweat slides down the middle of my back. I think of all those stories you hear about people who have hard childhoods who leave home the minute they can and never go back. I do the math in my head. Three years to graduation. A long time before I can go anywhere.

I take a deep breath and remember that I am different now. Maybe if I try hard enough, I won't have to be one of those runaway people.

I bring my hand to my face and pull away tiny pieces of the jagged scab. My face reflects in the rounded airplane window, and I see it is now a tiny Massachusetts, with Cape Cod curling toward my ear. In only a few more days it will be gone. I feel the fresh, smooth parts and marvel at how soft they are. New skin amazes me. New skin is a miracle. It is proof that we can heal.

RESCUE MISSION #112 — EVERYBODY SEES THE ANTS

Granddad is being held captive by ants in party hats. They are playing Twister. Granddad is calling the colors. He cannot play because Twister requires limbs, and he is missing two of his—one arm and one leg this time.

"Left hand green!" he calls.

The ants twist around to make the play.

"Granddad!" I say.

He waves me in, and a chair appears to his right.

"Right foot red!" he says.

"You know the ants?" I ask.

"What do you mean?"

"I mean—aren't the ants in my head? Don't they mean I'm crazy?"

"Hell no. The ants are in everyone's head. Been in mine since I was a kid," he says. Then, "Right hand yellow!"

I can't wrap my brain around this.

"Everybody sees the ants?"

He looks at me and says, "Well, how many people do you think live perfect lives, son? Aren't we all victims of something at some time or another?"

"I don't follow."

"Left hand red!" he says. Two ants fall on this turn, and the ant laughter gets louder. "Well, think about it. How many bad things can be done to a person? You got murder and assault, rape and robbery for starters. Just with those, you're looking at some big numbers of how many people see the ants." He calls, "Left foot blue!"

I say, "Huh," because I'm not sure how many people he means.

"There's battery, conspiracy, extortion, slander, defamation and harassment, child abuse, stalking — the list is long, isn't it? Don't forget that every crime has hundreds of victims — everyone who knew and loved the victim and the criminal. That shit can trickle down."

"All those people see the ants?"

"Yep. Right hand green!"

"Wow."

"Yeah," he says. "If there *are* people who don't see 'em, I'd say we outnumber them a million to one."

PART THREE

Tragedy is a tool for the living to
gain wisdom, not a guide by which to live.
—*Robert F. Kennedy*

LUCKY LINDERMAN LOOKS SMALLER HERE

Dad picks us up and drives us away from the Philadelphia airport. He and Mom make small talk while I stare out the window. It's so humid here, I'm chilly. I have goosebumps.

About ten minutes after we start driving, Mom says, "So did you do it?"

Dad keeps his eyes on the road. "Do what?"

"The thing you said you'd do?"

"I don't recall saying I'd do anything."

Mom stares at the side of his head. The ants hand her an auger so she can drill right into his skull. It takes a hundred of them to carry it over the seat back.

"Did you talk to the McMillans?" she says.

"No."

Mom's face puckers into a cinched bag of disappointment.

"What could I say to them?" he says. "I mean, obviously the kid learns it somewhere."

"That's not my point."

"So what *is* your point?" he asks.

"You were supposed to do something."

Mom sighs and looks out the window as suburban Philadelphia sleeper towns race by. She doesn't say another word. I sit in the backseat and watch Dad as he drives. The ants say: *You are not a turtle, Lucky Linderman.*

Dad parks in the driveway and says, "Welcome home!" Like a tour guide. As if we were just passengers riding on his shell.

I get the suitcase out of the trunk, and I deposit it in the laundry room and go to my room. After I lie there for a while, I realize that Dad isn't ever going to do anything but be there to drive us home from the airport. And cook. And if I want something bigger to change, it's up to me. I'm scared shitless, yes. I'm doubtful, yes. But I'm angry. Angry that I am doing this because Dad can't. But then I sniff breakfast, and I know that Dad is doing what he can.

Once he's placed plates of steaming-hot pancakes in front of us, he arrives at the table. He looks at each of us for a long minute and smiles.

I want to tell him about Ginny and kissing and how I can bench-press sixty pounds. I want to tell him about how Arizona changed my life, but instead, because these are the best pancakes I've ever eaten, I say, "How did you make these pancakes taste so good?"

"Chef's secret," he says, and then tells me that the secret is lemon zest.

Mom says, "Did you know Lucky is a great cook?"

Dad raises his eyebrows.

"He even taught Jodi a few things."

Dad laughs. "Your aunt Jodi is a lost cause."

I sit up proudly. "I got her to eat brie."

Dad smiles at me. I suddenly feel so stupid for giving up eating when I was thirteen. The ants say: *Forget about it. We're all larvae once.*

He says, "Well, if you could teach Jodi about cooking, you must have magical powers."

"I think he does," Mom says, and winks at him.

"So, what'd you think of Dave?" Dad asks.

"He's cool," I say. "He taught me how to lift weights, which was really good. But he works too much." Do they notice my smirk when I say this?

"True," Mom says.

"And Aunt Jodi is nice, but she's nuts. I mean that in a nice way. But she's nuts."

"No doubt," Dad answers. Mom nods.

"Lucky met some nice friends out there, didn't you?" Mom says.

"It was good."

"Glad to hear that," Dad says. "Good to see you smiling."

Good to see me smiling? Can this conversation be more weird? I want to give Dad a chance, but if the changes that are about to happen in our family are going to be credited to my smiling, I will be irked. So I decide now is the time to say something.

"I'd really like to get some weights. I like working out." I say. They don't look up from their plates or say anything. I add, "It makes me feel better about being a Linderman."

"What the hell does that mean?" Dad asks. He stops eating his pancakes and glares at me.

"It means I'm tired of being me."

They stare at me.

"It means I'm taking control of my life," I say.

They stare at me and then look at each other.

"I think I know where I can get a weight set," Dad says. "I think a guy at work is selling one."

Mom's eyes are glassy. "That would be great, Vic."

Dad leans toward me and frowns with his eyebrows. "And there's nothing wrong with being a Linderman," he says. "We should be proud to be Lindermans."

I want to point out that he said "we" and not "you." I reach up and touch my Massachusetts scab, and I can't help but rub it a little. For all my talking, I'm still nervous. For all my lifting, I'm still weak. Right now, Dad is the least of my worries.

When I check in the mirror after breakfast, I see the scab has separated into a bunch of little scabs. It's Hawaii. The final scab on my cheekbone is Mauna Kea, Hawaii's tallest mountain. Kauai is about to flake off any minute now. Maui after that. I predict that by tomorrow all physical traces of Nader will be gone. Then it's up to me to erase the brain traces — my mental scab.

RESCUE MISSION #113 — BANANA RAIN

I am in a pit thirty feet deep, alone. I'm in tattered black pajamas. I have sores on my feet. I'm missing my right arm and most of my teeth. I have a beard.

Someone calls, "Lucky?" over and over again from the top of the pit, but I can't see anyone.

"Meet me in the tree, son. Remember?"

I sit in the mud and meditate. Breathe in. Breathe out. I see myself in the tree with Granddad Harry. But when I open my eyes, I'm still in the pit by myself.

"Try again!" he says.

I try again. Open eyes. Still in pit.

And again. And again. It begins to rain. Bananas.

"Try again, Luck! Come on!"

The pit fills with bananas. They are Chiquita bananas — store-bought. They have stickers on them with clever sayings. Instead of meditating, I take some of the stickers and stick them to my sore skin. I do this until I realize I will soon drown in bananas if I don't get out of here. I try to climb on top of them. They mush under my weight, and make me sticky. Insects arrive.

I read the stickers. PLACE STICKER ON FOREHEAD. SMILE.

I have no problem placing the stickers on my forehead. But I cannot smile.

"Try again, Lucky! Don't give up! Get to the tree!"

I meditate, I breathe, I visualize, I *become* the fucking tree, but I can't get my ass out of the hole. I'm up to my neck in bananas.

"Smile, son! That's the ticket out!" I look up and see an outline of him — hazy and backlit. So far away.

My face is paralyzed. I can't smile. It's like all those times Mom told me that if I crossed my eyes too much, they'd get stuck that way. It's happened to my mouth. Operation Don't Smile Ever has rendered me frowning. Forever.

"Jesus, son! Hurry up!"

I keep trying, but my face won't obey. I think of cute things — puppies and kittens and babies — and happy things, like Ginny kissing me, and Granny Janice hugging me, and my ability to bench-press sixty pounds. I think about bad things that would make me happy — Nader in pain, Nader turning on Danny, Nader in jail. No smiles.

I have mere seconds left. I'm going to die by suffocation. Everything is black. My breathing is barely there. I hear muffled calls, but I block them out. I'm okay with dying in a pit of Chiquita bananas. I'm okay with everything right now. I'm at peace. Real peace.

Then I smile — unintentionally.

I'm in the tree with Granddad Harry. We're twins. We're both missing the same arm, have sores on the same feet; we stroke our beards the same way.

"Have you thought about my question?" he asks.

"Which one?"

"The one about why you come here. The time I asked you if you really thought you could take me back with you?"

I nod.

"You know you can't, right?" he says.

"Look. I have *reason* to be here. I was sent. It's *important*," I say.

He strokes his beard. I stroke my beard. We're like mirror mimes. Except my face is still covered in banana stickers. Except he's really him and I'm not really anyone.

"You're not coming *here*," he says. "You're escaping *there*. Big difference."

• • •

When I wake up, it's the middle of the night, and I lie in bed for a minute. My forehead feels odd, so I reach up and touch it and find it's layered in Chiquita banana stickers that say PLACE STICKER ON FOREHEAD. SMILE. I spend several minutes removing them. When I get to the final layer, I have to rip them off fast — like Band-Aids. I save one and stick it to the inside of my secret Harry box under my bed.

I look at the box — a lifetime of secrets — and I know the change I'm about to make is a lot more than lifting weights and smiling and all the surface bullshit. It's about something bigger, but I just don't know what yet.

OPERATION DON'T SMILE
EVER—FRESHMAN YEAR

It was my last monthly meeting with the guidance department. I was sitting in one of the itchy tweed chairs in the waiting area. About two minutes after I got there, Charlotte Dent came in, pulled two college catalogs from the bookshelf and sat at the big table. She'd been crying, made obvious by the watery mascara under her eyes. The guidance secretary wasn't there, and we were on our own, but I didn't have the guts to talk to her.

She looked up and stared at me, and I looked at my shoes. Then she pushed the catalogs out of the way and put her head in her arms, as if she was napping. But I heard sniffling.

"Are you okay?" I finally asked.

"Yeah."

"You don't look it."

She looked up from her arms and put on a huge goofy smile. "How about now?"

"Nope."

I moved over to the table and sat across from her.

"I want to make sure you're okay," I said.

"Why? You believe the stupid rumors?"

"No."

"Then why?"

"Because Nader McMillan used to bully me before he started bullying you," I say. "And your questionnaires are making me worry."

"My what?"

"You know — the questionnaires?"

She shrugged and made a face like she was genuinely clueless.

"In my locker?"

"I have no idea what you're talking about," she said, and then the guidance counselor called my name from her office door, and that was the end of it. All I could think about during the meeting was who? Who put them into my locker if Charlotte hadn't? I know I saw Charlotte putting the paper into my locker back in February, but maybe I was being deceived. Maybe Nader or Danny had a pink pen and knew how to do curlicue handwriting. Maybe I was just an idiot — again.

That day I got a new questionnaire in my locker. It was in pink ink, with the same curlicue writing. *If you were going to commit suicide, what method would you choose?* It read: *I'm okay. Thanks for asking.*

LUCKY LINDERMAN RETURNS

The first person I see at the pool is Danny, who flashes a quick smile before he gives me the finger as a joke. He's over by the bathroom door, scrubbing down the black rubber slip-proof mats. I follow Mom to a shady spot under a tree and proceed to lose any nerve I ever had in my scrawny, pathetic body.

While Mom sets up her chair and applies sunscreen, I sit cross-legged and look around the pool. It's early, and the pool is empty except for the swim team stragglers and a few lap swimmers. I look back at Danny and I think about what Ginny said to me: *Friends act like friends.* My stomach tightens.

Mom digs out her swim cap from our pool bag and fits it over her head. I decide that I want to swim some laps, too. So I do. Mom takes lane three and I take lane five and we swim.

At first my brain focuses only on what my eyes see. The black line, the blue bottom. The black caulk at the seams. The bubbles that my breath creates and the waves and currents of my arms and legs moving through the water. I can taste the chlorine and feel the pressure on my eyeballs. I can feel my scalp cutting through the water and my new cheek enjoying the cool, refreshing liquid.

After a while I get bored, so I dry off and sit on a bench in the sun and close my eyes and daydream about the new me. School is going to be different. Life is going to be different. I am going to be brave.

"Hey, dickhead!" Nader calls from the office door. "The nuthouse called. They want your mom back."

My stomach double-knots as I replay the last Freddy pool scene in my head — the scene in which Kim promised us "disciplinary action." Am I a fool to have believed that he'd be fired for what he did to me? Am I really still that naive? After all these years? I feel my red face and pick Maui off my cheek and flick it. Danny's head pops up behind the concession stand. Nader appears next to him, with a stripe of zinc oxide across his nose and a whistle around his neck. The ants roll out a tiny howitzer and begin to calculate coordinates.

I watch my mother do another slow lap of breaststroke, and I dream up ways I can just stop coming here. Before I manage to think up a foolproof excuse, Lara and her mom appear at the gate. Lara smiles my way and gives a halfhearted wave as her mother gives their cards to Petra and they walk to their usual space behind the trees near the volleyball net.

This intensifies the feeling that I have to get away from this place. If I have to be humiliated in a public place, that's one thing. But being humiliated in front of Lara Jones just sucks. I walk slowly toward them, even though I'm dreading the pity she's about to dish. We meet at her blanket.

"Hey!" Lara says. "You're back!" She's holding her library book with her finger in the page as a bookmark, as though she'd been reading the whole way to the pool.

"Yep. Here I am."

"Did you have a good time?"

"Yeah. I guess," I say. "It was hot, that's for sure." She nods and smiles. "Anything exciting happen while I was away?" I ask.

She nods and winks while her mouth says, "Nope. Nothing exciting." This means yes, but she can't tell me in front of her mother. She starts walking away from the blanket and says, "Are you okay? We were worried about you."

"Yeah. Thanks." We walk toward the tetherball pole, out of earshot. She keeps her finger in her book and hugs it to her chest.

"I was so glad to see your car in the parking lot again," she says, gesturing me closer to her. She switches to a whisper. She tells me Charlotte was there on Friday doing funny dives with her little brother. "Her bikini top came off again," she says. "And since Nader was the senior guard on duty, he made her get out of the pool in front of everyone. It was horrible."

"Shit," I say.

"I mean, she covered herself the best she could with her arm, but you know — it was still awful. My mom complained to the board of directors. A few people did. They want him fired. That guy is such a jerk."

"Yeah. A total jerk," I say. I feel bad now. I feel bad for not calling the cops when he beat me up three weeks ago. If I'd done it, none of that would have happened. We start walking back toward her mother, who is now looking at us with those eyes mothers have when they think their kids are experiencing puppy love.

"Do you want to play some gin later?"

"Yeah. Sure. I'd love to," I say. "Finish your book first. I can tell you're dying to get to the end."

"The next one is waiting for me at the library," she says. She opens the book and sits down in the shade of the surrounding trees. I think about Ginny and how she was the first girl I ever wanted to kiss. The ants make smooching noises as I realize Lara is the next girl I want to kiss.

I see Mom drying out in the sun on her beach chair. Her eyes are closed. I sit down next to her and say, "Hey."

"Hey."

"Did you see who's working today?"

She opens her eyes and squints around the pool grounds. "No."

"Nader McMillan."

She sighs.

"Doesn't seem like he got fired, does it?" I say, pointing to my cheek.

She shakes her head and swears under her breath. "That's my fault. Totally my fault, Lucky. I just—" Her voice wobbles a bit. "I just had so many other things going on."

"It's not your fault," I say.

"No. When you become a parent, you have certain responsibilities. Totally. My. Fault." She stresses each word with a hand motion.

Lara turns a final page of her book and reads it. She gets to the end, stares out into the blurry distance, sighs and then closes the book. Mom sees me watching this.

"Seriously, Mom. It's not your fault. It's not your fault he didn't get fired, and it's not your fault he's an asshole." I say. I scratch my itchy cheek, and the last of Hawaii — my cheek-bone Mauna Kea — peels off and lands on my leg.

She stares into space for a minute. "Did I ever tell you what my mother used to say about assholes?" Her voice is cheery, as if our conversation just rounded a corner.

I shake my head.

"She'd say 'The world is full of assholes. What are you doing to make sure you're not one of them?'"

I say, "Wow," because that's probably the coolest thing I ever heard.

"Anytime any of us stepped out of line, she'd say that to us." She shakes her head. "The woman was a saint."

I meet Lara under the pavilion for a two-out-of-three gin match an hour later. She beats me the first time. I get totally lucky the second time and am dealt a near-winning hand. We sit there for a while between games, watching the scene together. The day-camp kids have complete control of the deep end now. Mom is over at our blanket, and I watch her call out to Kim the manager and stand talking to her for a few minutes.

I can tell from Kim's body language that she is apologizing. I can tell from Mom's body language that she is quoting her mother: *What are you doing to make sure you're not one of them?*

Tonight for dinner Dad makes a particularly scrumptious batch of barbecued ribs, and he lets me grill corn on my own without telling me how to do it better. I eat like a caveman. He makes a few jokes about his workday, and Mom laughs. She complains about the day-camp kids taking over her precious lane three, and he makes fun of her for ever thinking it was her lane to begin with. I listen and just eat and eat and eat.

"I think the McMillan kid might get fired tomorrow," Mom says.

"About time," Dad says.

They look at me, and all I can do is smile.

I'm not really smiling about Nader getting fired. I'm smiling because I feel like I'm part of a normal family. Sure, my father is still mostly turtle. And my mother is still going to keep swimming laps to appease her pool god. But *I* feel normal now. Not sure why. Not sure I should care why. I just do. I am so satisfied by this, and by the larger-than-usual portion of ribs I had for dinner, that I fall asleep early, before the *FMC* hour on the Food Channel, and I steer myself to Granddad Harry.

RESCUE MISSION #114—FIXING VIC

I see us from a distance at first. Granddad and I are in the tree, swinging our legs. Limb check: all present. He's smiling with the few teeth he has left, and I'm smiling, too. I can't hear what we're talking about, but I know it's good.

Then I zoom in and Granddad says, "You are a fine father to my son," which takes me a while to process. He means I'm being the father to my father that Granddad never was. "Thank you," he says.

We're silent for about five whole minutes as we watch the sun dapple spots on the jungle floor, and the canopy above us sways with the breeze.

"I feel very fortunate to have had these years with you," Granddad Harry says.

"Me too."

"Watching you grow into a man has been the best experience of my life," he says.

I feel hairs growing on my chest instantly. My sperm count increases. I say, "I figured out what to do about Nader McMillan."

"I see."

"I'm going to talk to him. Face him, you know?"

"Your grandmother would be proud. She was always the vigilante in our family."

At the thought of her, I sadden. "She missed you so much," I say.

"I'll see her soon," he says. "She'll be happy we fixed Vic."

Suddenly I'm by myself again, walking down a jungle path. I'm thinking: *Did we fix Vic? How?* I look up to the branches above me and can't find Granddad anywhere.

THE LAST THING YOU NEED
TO KNOW—MISSING LIMBS

I take an extra-long shower and concentrate on myself in the mirror once the steam dies down. I feel like my dream last night aged me. I look for proof on my face—all I find is the same fuzzy upper lip I've had all year. My cheek scar stares at me. It tries to remind me how weak I am. I block it out.

When I'm dressed, I find Mom in the kitchen, slicing pickles.

"Do you want to go to McDonald's for breakfast?" she asks, and I nearly fall over. Lindermans do *not* eat at McDonald's.

"Seriously?"

"I hear the coffee is better now. It used to be like drinking thinned tar."

I'm not used to this yet. I'm not sure I can pull off being normal.

Dad used to tell me about the guys at the VFW who could feel their amputated limbs. I feel like one of those guys—wiggling my weak, tortured, pathetic self from only a month ago even though I've amputated him.

It's a little like being two people at once. One minute I feel like the old Lucky who had nothing, and the next minute I realize I have everything I could possibly need.

While I'm in the driveway, I hear the neighborhood kids playing. Normal kids doing normal things. They probably haven't heard about the Vietnam War. They probably don't know that as of today more than 1,700 servicemen have still not been accounted for. They probably don't know that about 8,000 are still missing from Korea, or that approximately 74,000 never surfaced after World War II. They don't know that amputees sometimes try to wiggle limbs they lost.

I don't envy them. They have a lot to learn.

Mom orders a Sausage McMuffin with Egg, and I order an original Egg McMuffin with hash browns, and we park in the shade and as we eat, we try to figure out exactly how many laps we'll have to do to burn the delicious goodness off of our bodies.

When we get to the pool, Mom stuffs her hair into her swim cap and goes straight to the deep end. She waits until I get there and stares down the length of lane three. She says, "How many laps do I have to swim to work off that Sausage McMuffin?"

"A hundred," I say. "And another twenty for the sweet coffee and half of my hash browns."

"Wanna race?"

She's never asked this before. I know I will lose. But I get into position at lane four. She says, "On the count of three. One. Two. *Three!*" and we dive.

The sun hits the water and makes the bottom a mosaic of light. I can see my own shadow, racing through the wet, and I try to catch up with myself. I do not come up for air until I've done eight strokes. I picture being chased by a man-eating shark. I breathe to the right so I can't see Mom. This really isn't a race. It's the most fun I've had since Ginny dragged me around her shadows at night.

We stop racing at lap ten. I feel as if my lungs are on fire. Mom is equally winded, and we don't talk as we squat in the shallow end, catching air. I see Danny peeking out from the snack bar and I think — if it makes me a mama's boy to have fun racing my mom in the pool, then I'm Lucky Linderman, mama's boy. If it makes Lucky Linderman a fag or a dick or any of those other stupid names I've been called my whole life, then fine. I am a dick, a fag and a douche bag, loser asshole mama's boy.

Mom and I go for twenty nicely paced laps, and when I stop to catch my breath again, I see Lara and her mom setting up over by the picnic table and I wave. Lara waves back and smiles. She walks over to the pool and sits on the edge, with her feet in the water.

"Did you hear?"

I make the *no, I did not hear* face.

"They fired Nader McMillan last night."

I look at her and tilt my head. If it makes me a fag to think her cheekbones are the most amazing things I've ever seen, then I am Lucky Linderman, fag. Because her cheekbones are monumental.

"That's awesome," I say, but I'm still thinking about her cheekbones.

"I'm so relieved," she says. "If he could do that to Charlotte and get away with it, then he could do it to any girl at this pool."

I nod and stare at her perfect, shiny round shoulders, and I can barely think straight. She walks back to her book and her mother in the shade, and the ants say: *What do you have to lose, Lucky Linderman?*

At lunchtime Mom and I sit on our blanket and munch chilled egg salad sandwiches. The ants sit on the corner of our blanket and play poker. They bet with crumbs.

Mom does a few more laps, though the pool is so full of day-camp kids, there's really no point. She gets out, dries herself off and starts to pack up. It's three thirty. We're going home early to eat dinner with Dad, because that's the new plan. More family dinners. More time away from Bistro La-Di-Da for Dad, which just might mean more happiness for all of us. Or not, I guess, depending on how open Dad really is to the new plan. Either way, I feel so full of Aunt Jodi's positive chi I could choke. I say good-bye to Lara, but she's so into her new book she doesn't even look up at me while saying, "Yeah, see ya."

As Mom pulls out of the lot, I see that Nader McMillan is

at the front gate, talking to the other guards. I want to crouch down in the car until Mom drives past him. I really don't think I can do this. My guts twist. We've almost driven past him when I say, "Can you stop for a sec? I need to take care of something."

Mom stops on the shoulder of the road, and I get out of the car and walk over to the front gate.

Nader sees me coming. For once he doesn't have something smart to say. He's just watching me come at him. My back is straight. I look him in the eye. He takes a step away from his lifeguard friends, and when I get there, he's standing, arms crossed, smirking at me.

I say, "We need to talk." My heart is totally beating out of my chest. I bet he can see it.

He nods. "Yeah?"

I get right in his face—as much as I can considering I'm about six inches shorter than he is. "Here's the deal," I say, and I poke him in the chest. "You're not going to give me any more shit."

"I'm not, huh?"

"Nope. And if you lay a finger on me again, I'm calling the fucking cops on you."

"Oh, really?"

"Yeah. And if I see you doing your fucked-up, perverted shit to any other kids? I'm going to call the cops then, too."

He's looking at me like back when we were pretend-friends—he's smiling a little. He says, "Who loaned *you* a set of balls, banana boy?"

I poke him again — this time with two fingers. "Save it for a kid who gives a shit."

"You think you're tough now?"

"You just don't scare me, that's all." My heart, now beating four times faster than it was only thirty seconds ago, would disagree, but I'm doing okay.

"Huh," he says. Then he takes a step toward me and gets right in my face.

Rather than step back, I lean toward him so he can feel my breath. "I'm serious," I say. "I'll put your ass in jail. Don't think I won't." I give him a crazy-looking, bugged-out-eyeball stare and say, "I'll tell them everything if I have to."

He puts his hands up in that joking defensive way. "Okay, man. Whatever you say."

He's still giving me that cute and cocky look right up close — as if he's about to laugh. But I don't care. Now that I've said it, it's over. My part is over until I have to keep my word... which I will do if I have to.

Kim the manager says, "McMillan, get what you came for and get out of here. If a board member sees you, it'll be my ass."

I stand right there — in his face — until he slinks off to the chemical shed to get the stuff he came for. I feel amazing. I feel everything.

As I'm walking back out the gate, Ronald struts in. Fast. He walks over to Danny, who's standing outside the snack-bar window, and he picks him up by his shirt. "Where's McMillan?"

Danny just blinks. Ronald grabs his face and squeezes. "Where *the fuck* is McMillan?"

"Chill out, man," Danny says, and points to the chemical shed. I stop and turn back around. Charlotte is walking slowly down the sidewalk outside the fence—and is just passing Mom's car. She's on her cell phone. I bet she's calling 911, because Ronald's hawk tattoo is three-dimensional with crazy.

I try to think up a way to stop Ronald from doing what he's about to do. I want to tell him that it's not worth it. That he might go to jail for some little shit like Nader. But Ronald is too fast, and I end up standing there staring at him run-walk to the shed.

All I can do is hope he doesn't hurt Nader too much. And I really can't believe, after everything Nader's put me through, that I'm actually hoping that. But I am.

Charlotte closes her phone and stops to look through the chain-link fence. Ronald has disappeared into the chemical shed. Then we hear the violent noise.

It's pounding, rhythmic and loud. The whole shed is shaking. A minute later Ronald appears. He has blood on his chest, smeared over part of his tattoo, and he's covered in a shiny layer of sweat. I walk to Mom's car and before I open the door, I say to Charlotte, "You okay?"

She nods, and I sit into the car and nod back.

Mom and I get home at 3:40 to find that Dad has already minced garlic and chopped chives. He's sliced the chicken breasts into chunks—perfect one-inch cubes. He's twisting a lemon over an old glass juicer that Granny Janice used to use to make my orange juice.

"Good day at the pool?" he asks.

"The McMillan kid got fired," Mom says. "So that was good." She leaves out any mention of my facing up to Nader, and I'm glad.

Dad nods.

"And Mom and I raced."

"Who won?"

We laugh. Mom puts her hand up.

"And Lucky played card games with his girlfriend most of the afternoon."

"I lost them, too." Mom makes a mental note that I did not correct her. I make a mental note to make Lara Jones into my girlfriend as soon as I can.

Dad says, "Women, son. Get used to losing." He goes back to twisting lemons.

"Can I help?" I ask.

"Nah. I got it covered."

I stand around for a minute or two, but he's not saying anything to me, so I go to my room and change and come back out when I hear Mom is out, too.

"You don't have to help if you don't want to, but I could use a hand with this rice," Dad says. Mom looks to me.

"Sure," I say.

"Don't let it boil over while I get these on the grill."

When he goes out, Mom looks at me and half smiles. I think we both know we can't work miracles on Dad.

"You know, this is fun," he says as he walks back in through the kitchen door.

Mom and Dad exchange a look as if they have some sort of secret. Mom leaves the kitchen and claims she has to do something out in the front yard. Definitely one of the weirder things she ever "had to do."

Dad doesn't say anything. He starts looking for something else to do for dinner, but everything is in that in-between stage. After watching him search for a few more seconds, I take a deep breath and say, "You okay, Dad?"

He jumps a little. "Yup, chicken should be ready to turn in a minute."

I keep looking straight at him. He's weirded out by it. He starts poking around, opening and closing cupboards, not looking at me. He moves some dishes from the right-hand side of the sink into the left-hand side. Then he looks at his watch. I'm about to ask him again when he says, "You know, this place wasn't the same without you guys around." My heart lifts. Then he kills it a little. "I didn't have anybody to cook for," he adds with a smile.

"Better get used to it." I sigh. "I can cook for myself now, you know."

He finally looks back at me and I see he's all soft — just like the day Granny Janice died. He says, "Are *you* okay, son?"

I nod. When he doesn't say anything else, I say, "Yeah. I'm okay."

He looks into my eyes for a second and nods, subtly. Then he gets up and goes to turn his kebabs. I feel kind of sorry for him for some reason, and then the feeling passes and I go back to wondering just how badly Ronald hurt Nader and trying to figure out how I feel about it. It's easier than figuring out how I feel about Dad.

A little while later we're sitting around the plastic deck table on the back porch, eating my favorite yogurt-chicken-pineapple-tomato-on-rice dish, listening to our neighborhood. Parents come home from work. Kids come home from day camp or day care or wherever they were shipped off to. The smell of a hundred dinners wafts through our backyard. We don't say much. None of us looks worried.

After dinner Dad goes back to work and promises Mom he won't be home too late. I watch two shows on the Food Channel and then go into my room and lie down on top of my POW/MIA comforter. I think about the last month of my life—from getting my Ohio scab to meeting Aunt Jodi, loving Ginny, loving and hating Uncle Dave, facing Nader, appreciating my mom and dad and discovering Lara—and I feel lucky.

Before I know it I'm almost asleep, wrapped in a cozy feeling of contentment. I can feel that my hands are behind my head. I have *lounged* myself to sleep. I smell the chlorine from my skin and feel the heat where the sun kissed me today. My muscles are slightly sore from racing. It's a satisfying ache.

RESCUE MISSION # 115

We're in the camp where we first met, by the stream where I fell. I am a grown man, not a teenager. I have the beginnings of a beard, and my hair is too long. I sit on a big rock, and Granddad sits on the rock next to me. He folds his hands into each other and leans his elbows on his knees.

"Hey, kid," he says.

"Hey, Harry," I answer. I don't think I ever called him Harry before.

"Wanna take a walk?"

I'm watching the clear stream travel by and am comfortable. I say, "To where?"

"Somewhere special," he says.

I reach into my breast pocket and retrieve a pack of cigarettes. I've never smoked in my dreams before. I offer him one and he takes it. He's never smoked in my dreams before, either. We smoke and watch the water flow by.

"You're good to your dad," he says. "I was afraid he'd grow up to be an asshole without me." He takes a drag. "Many a night I lay here wondering if Janice's soft side would ruin him."

"Nah — he's a good guy," I say.

"You happy these days?"

"Yeah." I take a long drag and think of Ginny. "I think I'm figuring it out. You know — how to be happy."

He digs out a fortune cookie fortune from his mouth, as if his mouth has a pocket. It says THE SIMPLEST ANSWER IS TO ACT. He hands it to me. I nod and put the fortune in my own mouth pocket. He reaches into his mouth pocket again and retrieves a ring. It's gold — his wedding band.

"Wear that," he says.

"Okay," I answer, and I slip it onto my finger.

He puts out his cigarette in the mud bank, and I do the same. He turns and says, "Come on. I want to show you this."

We walk on the jungle path, and I can tell he has no fear of Frankie or any other guards. I do a quick limb inventory — he's got them all. So do I.

"Where's Frankie?" I ask.

"He went home to his family," he says. "Left me here to die."

"Oh," I say. Then I stop walking, and add, "To die?"

He stops and looks back at me on the path. "Did you think I'd live forever?" he asks.

We arrive at the makeshift jungle prison. He's made it his own. There is an American flag flying. There is a real bed, not just a few bamboo crates. Sitting in the chair where Frankie used to sit is Granny Janice. She waves.

I wave, even though I want to run into her arms and breathe in her baby-powder smell. I say, "Hi, Granny."

She says, "I'm so glad you could make it, Lucky."

I ask myself: *Make it to what?*

Granddad is at the back door — the one that leads uphill. He's urging me to follow. We walk for about twenty minutes in silence. We hold hands. At the top of the hill, where the view would make anyone wonder why Earth allows us to continue living here and ruining it, there is a hole. It is six feet long and about four feet deep. Next to the hole is a pile of dirt and a shovel.

"I need you to tell your father that everything is over now. I need you to tell him that I loved him more than I ever loved anything in my life."

I'm crying. I can't talk. I nod.

"I need you to tell him. You will, right?"

I sniffle. "Yes. I'll tell him."

He jumps into the hole like a man who is not dying. "If my government ever wants to know where I am, you tell them I died where the view was outstanding."

I squeeze my eyes shut and quietly sob for all of us. For him, for Granny Janice and for Dad. I sob for Mom and how she married into this. I sob for myself. When I open my eyes, he is lying in the bottom of the hole, motionless. His arms are behind his head, and he has a grin on his face. He has *lounged* himself to death.

I cover him with the dirt. Time passes. I sweat through my shirt, and my beard itches. Only when I finish, I stab the shovel into the ground and find a cigarette and light it. I marvel at the view — a landscape of cloudlike jungle canopy. It is, without a doubt, outstanding.

• • •

When I wake up, it's dark. It's 3:34 AM. I'm covered in grit and sweat. My feet are brown with mud, and I'm sucking on something. I spit it into my hand and unfold it. It's a fortune from a fortune cookie. It says THE SIMPLEST ANSWER IS TO ACT.

I bend my thumb to my ring finger, and I feel it there — the wedding band. And so it's time.

LUCKY LINDERMAN HAS
SOMETHING TO SAY

There is something magical about the world at night. Sitting at the dining room table, sipping a glass of iced tea, I can totally understand why Dad gets up so early. Minutes seem to last longer when the rest of the world is asleep. I think he heard me come in here, because I hear him flush the toilet and walk down the hall.

He fixes himself a glass of ice water and sits down across from me.

How do I do this? How do I tell my father that I got to meet his father, when he didn't? That I just buried him? How do I explain something so unbelievable? So unjust?

I take the ring off and set it on the table between us.

He looks at me, still smudged with red dirt, my hair dried to my head. He picks up the ring and reads the inscription out loud. "'Harry and Janice, September twenty-third, 1970.'" He looks at me. "This is my dad's." He blinks. "Where did you get this?"

I say, "Do you have a few minutes?" I reach across the table and hold his hand. "I need to tell you something really important."

Results for Men Facing the Draft in 1971
Lottery Numbers, by Birth Date, for Selective Service—
Lottery Held July 1, 1970

This determined the order in which men born in 1951 were called to report for induction into the military.

	Jan	Feb	Mar	Apr	May	Jun	Jul	Aug	Sep	Oct	Nov	Dec
1	133	335	014	224	179	065	104	326	283	306	243	347
2	195	354	077	216	096	304	322	102	161	191	205	321
3	336	186	207	297	171	135	030	279	183	134	294	110
4	099	094	117	037	240	042	059	300	231	266	039	305
5	033	097	299	124	301	233	287	064	295	166	286	027
6	285	016	296	312	268	153	164	251	021	078	245	198
7	159	025	141	142	029	169	365	263	265	131	072	162
8	116	127	079	267	105	007	106	049	108	045	119	323
9	053	187	278	223	357	352	001	125	313	302	176	114
10	101	046	150	165	146	076	158	359	130	160	063	204
11	144	227	317	178	293	355	174	230	288	084	123	073
12	152	262	024	089	210	051	257	320	314	070	255	019
13	330	013	241	143	353	342	349	058	238	092	272	151
14	071	260	012	202	040	363	156	103	247	115	011	348
15	075	201	157	182	344	276	273	270	291	310	362	087
16	136	334	258	031	175	229	284	329	139	034	197	041
17	054	345	220	264	212	289	341	343	200	290	006	315
18	185	337	319	138	180	214	090	109	333	340	280	208
19	188	331	189	062	155	163	316	083	228	074	252	249
20	211	020	170	118	242	043	120	069	261	196	098	218
21	129	213	246	008	225	113	356	050	068	005	035	181
22	132	271	269	256	199	307	282	250	088	036	253	194
23	048	351	281	292	222	044	172	010	206	339	193	219
24	177	226	203	244	022	236	360	274	237	149	081	002
25	057	325	298	328	026	327	003	364	107	017	023	361
26	140	086	121	137	148	308	047	091	093	184	052	080
27	173	066	254	235	122	055	085	232	338	318	168	239
28	346	234	095	082	009	215	190	248	309	028	324	128
29	277	—	147	111	061	154	004	032	303	259	100	145
30	112	—	056	358	209	217	015	167	018	332	067	192
31	060	—	038	—	350	—	221	275	—	311	—	126

Source: Selective Service System

ACKNOWLEDGMENTS

First:

This book is in memory of Ed Daniels — a good man who cared about women and wasn't afraid to show it.

Second:

This book is dedicated to every missing soldier and to their families. I want to especially thank Jo Anne Shirley, vice chairman of the board of the National League of POW/MIA Families. Jo Anne, your frankness about what it's like to have a missing loved one was incredibly helpful and affecting. Additional thanks to the many people who talked with me about their own POW/MIA, Vietnam War and draft lottery experiences.

Third:

I owe planet-sized thanks to my agent, Michael Bourret, who is so tremendous they should make an action figure out of him. To the entire team at Little, Brown who do such amazing work, including my editor Andrea Spooner, who *understands*; Deirdre Sprague-Rice, who should be cloned; and Victoria Stapleton, who sent me a tweet while I was sitting on a bench by myself, which meant a lot more than she thinks it did.

I owe thanks to the usual suspects. My family — Mom, Dad, Robyn, Lisa and the whole extended crew for your support. And Topher, love — how do I thank you? Let me count the ways. My friends — a bow of gratitude to Krista, my superhero, and to Christine and Maria, who introduced me to the V-Day movement. Without you (and Ed) this book would not be. All other friends know who they are and should assume this sentence is for them. My fans — to every one of you who has written to me, come to see me at signings, or spread the word. And to the amazing educators, booksellers, librarians, teachers and bloggers who have supported my work, thank you so much.

And finally:
To my fellow kindness ninjas who help without saying a word — thank you. I see you. Do you see me?